Lady Bits

KATE JONEZ

TREPIDATIO
PUBLISHING

Trepidatio books may be ordered through booksellers or by contacting:
Trepidatio Publishing
www.trepidatio.com
or
JournalStone
www.journalstone.com

The views expressed in this work are solely those of the authors and do not necessarily reflect the views of the publisher, and the publisher hereby disclaims any responsibility for them.

ISBN: 978-1-947654-81-5 (sc)
ISBN: 978-1-947654-82-2 (ebook)
Trepdatio rev. date: March 22, 2019

Library of Congress Control Number: 2019931088

Printed in the United States of America

Cover Art: Mikio Murakami
Interior Layout: Jess Landry

Edited by Scarlett R. Algee
Proofread by Sean Leonard

For Matthew, the love of my life
who makes writing possible.

Lady Bits

CARNIVORES

ALL THE DAY YOU'LL HAVE GOOD LUCK

A THOUSAND STITCHES

EFFIGY

MOUNTAIN

FAIRY LIGHTS

BY THE BOOK

NO FEAR OF DRAGONS

LIKE NIGHT AND DAY

A FLICKER OF LIGHT ON DEVILS' NIGHT

THE MOMENTS BETWEEN

POOR ME AND TED

SILENT PASSENGER

RULES FOR LOVE

ENVY

ACCIDENTAL DOORS

Carnivores

Francie is mostly fine.

By Friday, if she's extra careful, she'll be able to get the lights cut back on. She'll have to make more in tips than normal. If that fails, she can shortchange the cash register. She's not proud she does that, but there are worse ways to get money.

She could ask her mother. She could, but that's not a thing that Francie's going to do. Not if she's starving. Not if she has to wear rags and fly a sign next to the highway begging for change. Not if she has to give five-dollar blowjobs. Nothing is worse than listening to her mother go on and on about how Francie would be better off if she came back home to Fayetteville.

Her little apartment over the laundromat gets scary at night without the electric. Drunks from the bar on the corner creep around in the alley to take a pee, or whatever it is they do down there. Francie has never gone downstairs to investigate. They're harmless, probably, even though it sounds like they're murdering each other with knives and broken bottles.

Even though her apartment has cardboard in one of the windows where glass should be and roaches that won't leave no matter how much they're poisoned and permanent mold in the bathtub and is crappy by anyone's standards, it's a hundred times better than sleeping in the park. It's hard to get clean enough in public washrooms to go to work. Everybody, even people who are nobody, think it's just fine to mess with a girl by herself who sleeps in the park.

Francie likes that the apartment is all hers, even if she doesn't have furniture or dishes or anything, and the lock on the door is a padlock she put there herself. More of a squat than an apartment, technically, but Francie isn't going to turn the landlord in. Probably they shouldn't be renting to an underage person anyway.

The apartment isn't so bad once the sun comes up. For a while in the morning, anyway, until the dryers in the laundromat get going. There's nothing as hot as Houston in summer over a laundromat.

Francie fills a spaghetti sauce jar she peeled the label off with bathroom water and trickles it over the Venus flytrap she bought at the Dollar General. She'd put a fly in its mouth about a week ago, but nothing much has happened. Her mother tells her she shouldn't get a dog because she can't even keep a houseplant alive. Francie is better at taking care of things than her mother even knows.

Francie waters the plant every day, but maybe the plant isn't going to make it. Its mouth is starting to look a little brown where the meat of the fly touches it, and its leaves are beginning to droop.

Francie nudges the clay pot with her hip. She feels a little twinge as she watches the plant sail through the air and smash to the alley below. She doesn't feel bad for more than a second, though. What she wants is a dog.

For good measure, she nudges the spaghetti sauce jar off the sill too. It smashes in the same general area as the potted plant. Francie hopes at least one of the drunks stumbles and falls on her broken glass. It's what they deserve for scaring her the way they do.

Tuesday is Francie's regular day off. On a day off back in Fayetteville, she'd probably go by Renton Park by the high school, find Curt or Anna or some of the others, maybe hang out in the Walmart parking lot, score some weed. She's not sure yet how she's going to spend her day off here. None of the people she works with seem like they'd want to hang out in a park. They're older, too, mostly in college. They'd probably figure out in no time that she used a fake ID to get the job.

Francie stuffs her work apron, two pairs of jeans, and all the panties she can find into her backpack. She unzips the cushion of the overstuffed chair and reaches into the opening she cut in the foam. She pulls out her money and peels off a twenty. It'll make the electric harder to pay for, but whatever, she's got to eat and do wash, right? She stuffs the money back in its hidey hole and zips the cushion closed, then heads out the door with her backpack slung over her shoulder.

The light is hazy, like it wants to rain but doesn't have the energy. There's a salty, fishy smell in the air even though it's two bus transfers and more than an hour to the ocean. The fake-flower smell of dryer sheets from the laundry machines almost drowns it out.

The brown dog with the gray muzzle and no collar noses around the laundromat dumpster.

"Hey, brown dog," Francie calls to him. He's not the kind of dog who gets a name. He's not a pet kind of dog.

He lopes over and gives her a sniff.

Francie squats down and scratches behind his chewed-up ear. The dog nudges her bag like he's asking if she's got anything for him.

Everybody wants something.

He's a nice enough dog, even though his breath smells like ass. She'll probably get him a hamburger or something later.

A gold car pulls into the parking lot of the laundromat. It's got that pearly look to the gold paint that expensive cars have. It doesn't fit in at the laundromat. Francie tries to look without being too obvious, to see who the driver is. The windows are tinted so much it'd be illegal in Arkansas.

The car pulls into a parking space and just sits there. The door doesn't open or anything.

Francie decides to ignore it. It's none of her concern if some rich person wants to park their car in a crappy neighborhood. She goes inside and dumps her clothes in a washer. She looks in the trash until she locates a few empty detergent bottles. She carries them to the sink and puts a little water in each one. There's enough soap to do her one little load. She hopes so, anyway, as she pours the soapy water into her machine.

Francie looks up as a shadow passes over her.

"Hey," a man says. He's good-looking in that way that sometimes people's dads are good-looking. He's got a tan like he meant to, not like he got it from working, and he carries a shiny leather briefcase. He doesn't have a laundry basket or soap or anything. Francie makes a mental note of this fact. Maybe he owns the place. Maybe that's why he's here. There's always a chance.

"Hey," Francie says; then she turns her attention back to her laundry. She wants to be polite. That's what any human being would do, but she doesn't want to encourage some guy who's old enough to be someone's father.

The man passes by.

Francie takes her twenty dollar bill to the change machine. "Damn," she whispers to herself. It only gives quarters. She only needs a few. Twenty dollars' worth is going to weigh her down.

Her clothes will be fine for a while, Francie thinks as she leaves the laundromat. If anyone wants to steal her work apron and a bunch of used panties, they probably need them more than she does.

Francie waits for a break in the traffic and sprints across the street. She ducks under the yellow and green canopy that shades the rows of rickety tables of the bodega or cantina or whatever it's called. She failed Spanish. She might have tried harder if she'd known she would end up needing it. The working guys drinking beer from bottles ogle her perfunctorily as she steps up to the window.

Not a lot of white girls come here for lunch. Francie feels kind of weird, like her head is too big for her body and everyone is staring at her, but it's not so bad. Eventually she'll become some anomalous blip in the corner, and everyone will go back to their business. Francie orders the tacos de conejo because it's the cheapest thing. Someday she plans to look that word up and find out what it is she's eating. She gives the guy the twenty and asks for two dollars in quarters. He comes back with her change and a cardboard boat with the tacos.

"Here you go, Rosita," the old guy who works at the window says. That isn't her name, but he calls her that every time. Francie doesn't hate it.

She finds an empty table and sits with her back to everyone. This isn't the smartest thing to do, she's learned from sleeping in the park. It's a good idea to keep an eye on the people around, but she just can't stand the thought of making eye contact with the half-drunk working guys. It's better to avoid their gaze. She'll turn invisible faster that way. She unwraps her tacos and begins to make a mental list of the kinds of dogs she'd like to have, in descending order.

"Hey," a voice comes out of nowhere.

Francie jumps and looks around.

The guy from the laundromat sits next to her. He places his briefcase on the ground between his feet. "Didn't I just see you at the laundromat?" He grins really big, like he knows her already. "Did you forget about your clothes?"

"Nope." Francie scoots her chair over so they aren't sitting so close. She thinks about picking her nose so he'll leave her alone, but she doesn't. She does take a big bite and chew with her mouth open, though.

The old guy at the window gives Francie a concerned look.

Francie shrugs to let him know it's okay. It's probably okay.

"So, I bet you're wondering what it is I want to talk to you about," the man says. His smile hasn't faded at all. It's not a bad smile. His teeth are nice and white. His gums aren't all puffy and pulled back from the teeth like most old guys' are.

"Yep," Francie says. A sprinkle of lettuce falls on her shirt.

"I'm Edward, by the way." He holds his hand out to shake.

Francie ignores it for as long as she can stand it, but the guy doesn't relent. Finally, she gives in and shakes his hand. His hand is warm but not sweaty. Thanks to her it's a little greasy now. Very few people would wait it out like that. She can't decide if that's a character strength or a flaw. She's almost curious now about what words this guy's going to use, what angle he's going to come from, to tell her what it is that he wants.

"Want some?" Francie nudges the tacos in Edward's direction.

"No thanks," he replies.

Francie isn't all that hungry anymore. She picks the meat out and wraps it in paper for the brown dog and stuffs the package in her pocket. "What is it you want, then?" She hates that she had to ask. It makes her feel like she's got a few bad cards in a game of gin.

"I've got something I want to show you." Edward says this like he thinks Francie's going to like whatever it is.

Francie is pretty sure that she's not. It's just a matter of time before he pulls his dick out. She's pretty much sure about that. That's not the worst thing that could happen.

"What," she says, wanting to get it over with so she can get back to her laundry.

To her surprise, Edward leans down and grabs his briefcase. He places it on the table and opens the latches with a click. Looking from side to side, he whispers, "Just take a peek. I don't want everyone to see." He opens the briefcase just a crack.

Francie looks inside. There are rows and rows of bundles of bills. She can't tell the denomination, but even if there are only ones, it's still a lot of money. With that kind of money she could get any kind of dog she wanted. She could get more than one. She could maybe even move into a bigger apartment with a yard.

Edward closes the briefcase. "Well?"

"Well what?"

"What do you have to say?"

Francie shrugs.

"I want to give you that money," Edward whispers in her ear.

"What for?" Francie is trying to anticipate his next move. This is not the usual modus operandi, but it's related. Of this she is sure. She isn't sure yet if she's going to do what he asks. She'd like to have all that money, but she isn't going to do anything crazy.

"I want to hire you." Edward barely breathes the words. It's clear to see he's excited by what he's saying. There's a tremor in his voice. "Can we go somewhere to talk?"

Francie studies him for a minute, pretending she's sizing him up. That's not what she's doing, though. She did that a long time ago, back when she first spotted his pearly gold car. He could be a father to a girl just like her. He could be a soccer coach or a math teacher or a pastor of a church. He could have been a nice man if that's what he wanted to be. Maybe he is a nice man and maybe he's not. Whatever he is, he's not as good at making deals with people as he thinks he is. He's not dangerous, although maybe he wants to be.

"My apartment is across the street," Francie says. She tells him this although he already knows. She wonders how long he's been watching her. She wonders if he knows about the drunks who make all the noise at night in the alley.

Edward pretends to be surprised by her words. "You live there alone?" The tremor in his voice wavers like the vibrato on a violin.

"Yep." Francie gets up from the table. She might like to have three dogs and maybe a rabbit. Would the dogs eat the rabbit? Maybe an animal can be trained to go against its nature. Or maybe she'd keep the rabbit in a hutch. She makes her way out from under the awning and waits at the curb for a break in the traffic. She darts across.

Edward takes a minute to gather his things. He has to wait for the traffic to clear again, which gives Francie enough time to run away if that had been a thing she'd planned to do. She's not going to run away, though. It would drive her crazy to never find out what this guy wants.

By the time she gets to the door of her apartment, he's by her side. She opens the door and indicates that Edward should go up.

Francie slips the padlock through the hasp and spins the wheel.

She sprints up the stairs past Edward, who's only halfway up.

His breathing is a little labored. He looks like someone who goes to a gym, or at least has a treadmill at home. Seems like he'd be in better shape. He *is* old, though.

"You don't have any furniture," he says, looking around the room and trying to hide his distaste. The threadbare carpet and old-fashioned wallpaper probably don't look all that appetizing to someone who's used to nicer things.

"I have a chair," Francie says. "You can sit in it if you want."

"That's okay." Edward plops down on the floor and sits with legs crossed. A single roach makes its way through the fibers of the brown carpet. He doesn't see it.

"Sit." He pats the floor next to him. "I want to tell you about the job." He clicks the latches on the briefcase and flips it open.

Some of the bundles are twenties, others are hundreds. There's no guarantee they're the same all the way through, but still, this is the most money Francie has ever seen in one place. She'd definitely like to have this money. In a corner of the case there's a bag that closes with a zipper. That's the thing to watch; Francie makes a mental note. "I have a job," she says.

"This one is better." Edward grabs the zipped case like he's going to open it, then he puts it down again.

"Better how?"

"This," Edward waves his hand over the money, "is just a down payment."

"Oh yeah?" Francie is a little surprised that he hasn't shown her his dick yet. Maybe he really is a nice man. Maybe, but probably not.

"Did you ever want to be an actress?"

"No." Francie says. That's the absolute last thing she ever wants to be. She hates when people look at her.

Something flickers behind Edward's eyes. He wasn't expecting that answer.

"You're a natural." Edward's smile is turned all the way up again. "You'll make a fortune for us—and for yourself, of course."

"Who's 'us'?" She's absolutely certain that there's no one else aware of this plan. Except maybe a wife somewhere who's going to be pissed when she finds out her husband is screwing around with all the money that's supposed to be in their bank account. Or maybe he got it from selling his dead parents' house. Francie's mom had a whole bunch of money when she did that.

"The company I represent produces films for the overseas market. We'll provide you with an apartment and a generous salary. You'll sign a three-year contract and we'll be the sole owner of your image for that time frame only. The legal issues will be handled by our lawyers and you won't have to pay for a thing, not even legal fees."

He says the words like he practiced them a lot in front of a mirror. Their meaning is a jumble to her. It's like listening to a story from someone who's really into a specific thing. The way someone who's really into smoking weed tells a story about a baseball game and makes it all about how much weed he smoked. Why would she even care about who pays for legal fees? That's obviously something that Edward cares about, so he added it to his story. She's beginning to suspect this is the first time he's ever tried to do this thing he's planning to do. That might be better, might be worse. Francie can't decide.

"Naked, right?" Francie asks. "I have to be naked?"

"Not if you don't want to," Edward says. "Do you have a nice dress and high heels?"

"Not really." And by this, Francie means no. She's got zero use for clothes like that.

"Don't worry about that." Edward unzips the bag and slides out a silver cigarette case. "We'll go shopping and get you all the nice things you want."

Francie tinkers with the idea of shopping for all the nice things she wants. A really comfy bed might be nice, with silky sheets and puffy pillows. A toaster, a shower curtain, lots of toys for the dogs...

Francie tries, but she can't see what else awaits her in the zippered bag.

Edward opens the case. On one side is mirror; on the other there's elastic holding a glass vial with a black lid, a golden straw that's the same exact color as his car, and a razor blade. "Do you like coke?" He unscrews the vial and tips its contents onto the mirror. He tap-taps the mirror with the razor blade.

If Edward had done his homework, he would have known that Francie likes molly but not all that much. Edward seems lost in his fantasy about what a girl like her would be like. He has no idea about the real thing. He probably doesn't want to know.

"I guess," Francie says.

Edward puts the straw to his nose and snorts up one of the lines. He holds the straw out to Francie.

She takes it from him and stares at the little mound of white powder. She's pretty sure this will make her sneeze. With her other hand, she takes the silver cigarette case.

"Go ahead. It won't bite you." Edward's eyes are glassy. He looks excited and happy.

Francie drops the straw and grabs the razor blade. In a single smooth gesture, she plunges it behind his ear and drags it around to his Adam's apple. The razor is sharp, sharper than it needs to be. It slices through skin and muscle and veins like the meat had been cooked.

Francie jumps to her feet to avoid the spray.

It takes seconds for Edward to realize what has happened. Seconds more for him to convince himself it's true. His hands fly to his wound. Blood bubbles through his fingers. He seems disoriented and panicked. Probably the effects of the coke. Words spill from his mouth, but they don't make sense. He's not going to get any of the things that he's asking for. He stumbles to his feet, then to the stairs. He leaves a mess like the old carpet, in all its years of service, has never seen.

Francie goes into the bathroom and washes her hands. She listens to Edward over the hum of the dryers from the laundromat below. The apartment is really starting to warm up now that the sun is rising in the sky.

Edward's stream of incoherent words sputters to a stop. He's ceased rattling the door that won't open no matter how hard he tries. He falls with a thud, and the only sound is the hum of the dryers.

Francie unzips the bag. Inside there's a point-and-shoot camera, a dildo twice as big as any penis ever needed to be, a roll of duct tape, and several zip ties. It's not proof he's a bad, bad dude, but it'll have to be close enough.

The exact same thing about Francie that caught Edward's eye is exactly the thing that will keep her free. Francie gathers up Edward's money, rolls it in bundles, and stuffs it in her boots until no more will fit. She peels back the plastic on her ID and takes out her picture. The actual picture of the real Francie McClure looks back at her, as ordinary as any driver's license photo ever. She tosses the ID into Edward's open briefcase and throws in a pair of panties for good measure. She doesn't take anything with her, because she doesn't have anything to take.

Maybe Edward never once did the thing that Francie is one hundred percent certain he'd been planning to do. Maybe he was just working up his nerve to get going, or maybe he's done it a lot and ended a whole bunch of girls who never got to do all the things they wanted. Girls who never got the chance to grow up or have a dream come true or even get a dog. It's exactly the same to Francie, and she doesn't feel even the tiniest twinge of regret.

She makes her way down the stairs, avoiding the mess Edward made, and spins the dials on the combination lock. When she steps through the door and out into the parking lot, the haze has grown even heavier, but still it hasn't started to rain. The gold car with the pearly paint sits in the laundromat parking lot, looking so out of place that it's sure to draw attention to itself before long.

It won't take much to find old Edward once they locate the car.

"Hey, brown dog," the girl calls out. The brown dog with the gray muzzle lopes over and she scratches him behind his chewed-up ear. The girl reaches in her pocket and pulls out the meat from the taco she saved for him. The brown dog gobbles the conejo, whatever that might be, and wags his tail even though he seems out of practice.

The girl waits for a break in the traffic. The brown dog stands at her side. Together they sprint across all the lanes and begin the long journey to the next town and the next town and the next.

All the Day You'll Have Good Luck

The sun sinks down behind a bank of puffy lavender clouds that are much prettier than dusty old broke-down Frederick, Oklahoma, deserves. The carnival lights come on all at once, like a mad scientist flipped one of those old-timey switches. This is the part of day I like best. Not too early; not too late.

There's something about the way the yellow, red, and white lights stand out against the sky that makes the scene feel more special than it is. Like this is a moment captured for a postcard that's going to be sold at the newsstand up at the rest stop by the highway.

Dear whoever: Wish you were here, wrote no one ever who passed through Frederick.

From up on the little swell behind the closed-down Ace Hardware where I'm watching for my cue, I catch sight of my mom leaning over the railing and waving to Lainey on the Dumbo ride. Even with Baby June, who obviously is not a real baby, on her hip she's still the best-looking woman in the town. She takes a lot of care with her hair and makeup and wears stylish clothes that stand out from everybody else's. In Dallas, my mom says, nobody even notices. They know how to dress in Dallas. I wouldn't know. We stick to the small towns in Texas, Oklahoma, and sometimes Arkansas.

I wouldn't want to bother with fixing my hair and makeup, I don't think. Seems to me it's better just to blend in. Better to see than be seen.

The women in town say they hate my mom because she's not a good Christian. They don't even try to keep their feeling to themselves. They speak right up in line at Piggly Wiggly or when they're talking to each other at the Laund-O-Rama. Maybe it's true and Christians only like each other, but it's so completely obvious that they're jealous. The fact that Mom moved us in with the sheriff, Paul Ray Pearson, who up until recently was the most eligible man in town, doesn't help either. My mom knows all this and doesn't even care.

This whole situation, pretending we're the family of the sheriff, I can take it or leave it. It's not like it's a permanent thing. My mom isn't really going to marry Paul Ray likes he thinks she is. We aren't ever going to be his kids, no matter what. That's just not who we are. My mom tries and tries, but she's no good at the long game.

I like living in Paul Ray's house, I guess. I like having my own room, even if it did used to belong to Paul Ray's son Calvin and it's not really clear if I have to sleep on the couch when he comes back to visit. So far he hasn't come home, which makes me think he didn't move out of his own free will. The room, especially the closet and bed, smells like a cross between farm animals and bleach. It still has his football trophies on a shelf and posters of women in bikinis on the wall. I can't guess what it was that he did to get kicked out, but it must have been bad, because football players are loved more than Jesus in Frederick.

I found a box he must have hidden under his bed and forgotten about. It's got letters he wrote to a girl he was in love with. He's not much of a writer, but the feelings still come through. He loved her a lot.

From the words he used, you could tell he would have done anything to be with her. There's a picture of her that must be from when she was a little kid, because she looks way too young to be anyone's girlfriend. He's even got a lock of her hair. She must have loved him a lot too, because it's really thick. I wouldn't cut that much of my hair off for anyone. And a fingernail. A full fingernail, not a clipping. I feel like I know Calvin when I look in that box.

I see Calvin sometimes, before or after school in the seniors' parking lot. He sits on the hood of his truck and calls out to the senior girls as they walk by. They don't usually answer back. They hurry past him, in fact. Guys from the football team hang out with him sometimes. I think he brings beer. Calvin looks a lot like Paul Ray, except he doesn't have a pot belly. He's got muscles in his stomach that show when he lifts up his shirt, which he does a lot. It must be a nervous tic. Unlike Paul Ray, Calvin has lots of really nice long brown hair. I walk past him sometimes and wonder if he knows I sleep in his bed. He called out to me once, but I kept walking. I'm supposed to be invisible. It was weird being seen like that. I'm not from the town and I'm only thirteen. I could feel his eyes on me as I walked to class by myself. I thought about going back to sit with him on the hood of his truck. I thought about asking if I could have a beer, but I didn't, even though I always wanted to try drinking beer and cutting class.

I'm pretty sure Calvin doesn't go to school anymore. If I could, I'd get out of it too. I'm not doing good in school. At all. But living in a house means I have to go to school, even though that's just asking for trouble.

When I take a step, my flip-flops make a sticky noise on the black-top like a Band-Aid being pulled off. I walk fast, but keep it casual like I'm supposed to do. I like the sound of the ground kissing my feet. It's still hot in Frederick, Oklahoma, in spite of it being the end of September. The parking lot at the empty Ace Hardware is host to what's probably going to be the last carnival to come through town this year.

It's okay that carnival season is over. Frederick has high school football.

That's even better than this lame-o carnival that's only got kiddie rides and hardly any good games. High school football games are packed, and everyone is screaming and jumping around. That's perfect for me.

My mom thinks things in Frederick are grand. I think it's just a matter of time before someone catches on to us. She does the best that she can. That's what she says, anyway. Seems like a grownup would be able to look at the past and be able to see what's going to happen in the future. Seems like a grownup would be able to make a new plan and not just do the same thing over and over and hope things will turn out different. Maybe my mom is lying to herself. Maybe she's lying to us. I have to believe her, though. Who else am I going to believe?

My shadow spreads out before me, long and lanky as a willow tree. I wish I was my shadow and I could change shape as the sun goes down. Just at that moment, just as I'm thinking that thought, my flip-flop almost lands on a penny stuck in the tar. It's a good one, too. Heads up.

"Find a penny. Pick it up," I whisper as I squat down to get it. There's some more to the rhyme but I'm not sure what it is. I don't usually go to school, so there are a few holes in my education. The penny is stuck pretty good. I try to get my thumbnail under it and pry it up, but it won't budge. I would like my wish to come true.

"Pits," I say. It's my new favorite swear word. I like it because it sounds like a combination of *piss* and *shit* which are both pretty good swears. But *pits* is way better. When teachers get mad about cursing, there's not one single thing they can do about a word that isn't officially on the list of bad words. It's catching on around school. I even heard Calvin say it.

Lainey's first wail rolls across the parking lot. I jump up and leave the penny behind. I'm not in position. My mom is going to be seriously mad. I jog across the distance between me and my crying sister. The music from speakers that are supposed to be for tornado warnings sounds like the AM radio in our camper. The song might be saying something about love from spring to autumn, but the words are too muddy to tell for sure. It sounds different from the twangy guitar and slick voices that play in every store and restaurant in Frederick. It sounds like it's from some faraway place where people dress nice and speak with fancy language. Dallas, maybe.

I'm moving faster than I should, but chances are that nobody's going to notice me anyway. I'm not the kind of girl who gets noticed.

People are starting to gather around the pink elephant ride. The ride operator who seems like he's on the bad end of a hangover is looking at my mom with an expression that's melting from annoyed into scared.

Lainey is our screamer. She's my nine-year-old sister and she's got a natural talent for it. Even if we didn't have a use for her screaming, she'd still do it, I'm pretty sure.

She's sitting on the ground inside the gate, clutching her ankle. Her face is tear-stained and the smear of dirt across her cheek is convincing. The look on her face says she may never walk again. My mom, still holding Baby June, is cooing over her, pretending she's trying to get her to be quiet.

People are gathering around, trying to help. One thing I'll say for Oklahomans, they don't walk by people in trouble like they do in some other places.

I should be up there already. I jog a little faster. Just as I slide into place at the edge of the crowd, my mom makes eye contact. Her look is stern. It's a crack in the mask she wears when she's working. She reaches her arm out to help Lainey to her feet. Baby June clings to my mom like a trained circus monkey.

Just like she's supposed to, Lainey goes off like a siren. My mom adds her own hysterical voice to the din.

A man in the crowd flails his arms around. "Call an ambulance," he yells.

His words work like a magic spell to turn the pandemonium up a level. Perfect.

I snake through the crowd like I'm doing a ballet dance and slide my fingers into a wallet on this one, a purse on that. My mom says to only take cash, because we have to live in this town and there's no way we're able to use cards. I get one anyway. Never know.

"Stand back!" a man calls out. "Let me take a look."

I glance in the direction of the voice. Dr. Olney looks like every other old guy in town, with his starched plaid shirt and shiny cowboy boots, except he's got droopy eyes and extra saggy cheeks that make him look like a long-eared dog. He's the same doctor who checked Lainey out when the Summer Fun Fair came through Frederick back in July. Pits, this isn't good.

I snag two twenties with the tips of my fingers. They don't slide out like they should, and for a moment I'm exposed with my fingers wedged in the back pocket of a pair of black and white checked pants. The guy is squeezed into them as tight as a pork sausage in casing. I feel a little flutter in my chest, but I'm not really scared. I'm like a shadow. No one ever catches me. With a little tug the bills come free. The fat guy moves his arms like he's going to reach back, but he doesn't. I stuff the cash in my bra before I squeeze through the crowd to see what the doctor is doing. My mom can have the rest. This forty bucks is mine. I earned it.

Lainey's cute red curls are bouncing, and her big blue eyes are blinking and bleary but still incredibly china-doll pretty. She's howling and putting on her very best show for the doctor, who kneels down beside her and waves someone over from the crowd.

I could keep on working, but it's not such a good idea, since we aren't moving along to the next town. Even in Oklahoma, only so many crimes can get blamed on brown people. It's got to suck to be an honest person and have dark skin and always get blamed for everything whether you did it or not.

Don't crap where you eat, as Paul Ray says. He's always got something wise and insightful to say. Seems like someone so smart would be able to figure out what's going on right under his nose, especially since he's a sheriff and all. Men get all weird and dopey in the presence of a woman. My mom says that's the biggest advantage we have as females of the species.

She's always telling me I should learn to work it more. I don't see myself doing that anytime soon.

The doctor presses his fingers up and down Lainey's leg. He doesn't even look at my mom, like most guys do when they're supposed to be paying attention to us kids. He's intent and serious. "Broken," he says, and casts a glance designed to induce shame at the ride operator. "She's got to come in to the office so I can set it."

What the pits? Lainey's leg isn't broken. What's happening? This is not good. This is not good at all.

We need a distraction. It's obviously time to hit the road. We're not far at all from the patch of mesquite scrub where we hid our camper. I could probably see it from here if I was a couple of inches taller. I remember the first thing we saw when we got to Frederick was the back of the closed-down Ace Hardware. We could start the camper up before anyone even noticed. We could finally be on our way again. If ever there was a time for screaming, this would be it, but Lainey doesn't make a sound. I think about doing some screaming of my own, but I don't.

I see my mom looking into the crowd. Looking for me. I hunker down. I don't want to be part of this. That doctor must know Lainey's leg isn't broken. What are we supposed to do now? He's flushing us into the open like the hound dog he looks like. This isn't going to end well. A lump grows in my stomach like somebody kicked me.

"Move along, now. Nothing more to see." Dr. Olney hoists Lainey up and holds onto her without touching her leg.

The crowd disperses, and I lose my cover.

"Take care of June while I see to Lainey." My mom sets Baby June on the ground.

I search my mom's face for some clue about what I'm supposed to do. She's got on her working mask. It's smooth and calm. I can't detect a crack.

Baby June runs over to me. A few people glance at her sideways, because she runs like the seven-year-old kid that she really is. It's a weird thing to see. She's supposed to take tottering baby steps whenever she walks. My mom makes her practice it all the time and yells at her when she walks normal. Today she doesn't even notice June's walking wrong. This must be really serious.

Even though every one of the kids in my family has a different dad, we're the same because of how far away we are from ordinary people. Only with Baby June, it shows.

June is supposed to act like a baby, just like Lainey is supposed to scream and I'm supposed to move through a crowd like a shadow. Even if we wanted to, there's no way to change who we are. It's just a fact. Baby June hates it, though. She hates that she's never going to grow even one inch taller. I feel bad for her. How can she hate herself? That's just as bad as hating air or water.

My mom turns and walks along next to the doctor. The carnival lights flicker on them like lights from the sheriff's car.

Paul Ray Pearson will have to put my mom in jail when he finds out who she really is. He'll have to do it even if he loves her with all of his heart. He's a sheriff. That's what they do. Just like my mom is who she is. It seems kind of sad. We're all on a train headed for a cliff and nobody can do anything about it, no matter how much they might want to. I know my mom is trying to love Paul Ray Pearson back. It just isn't in her nature.

I'll have to take Lainey and Baby June and run away before they catch us and lock us up too. I could do it, but it won't be easy. I sure won't get caught and leave the little kids all alone to take care of themselves. It wouldn't hurt my mom to try a little harder. It's one thing to be who you are. It's another thing entirely to be lazy about it.

The music coming from the tornado speakers has horns and saxophones. It sounds slippery, like a fancy nightclub on TV. It's big-city music. Maybe I'll get as far away from Frederick and the stupid carnival circuit as I can and go see Dallas for myself. Baby June would like that. I can't say for sure about Lainey.

"Give me some money." June tugs on the hem of my shorts. "I want to play a game." With her other hand she rips out the ribbon that holds her hair in a ponytail on top of her head. Her fine black hair floats down around her shoulders.

"You know you're not supposed to do that."

June looks up at me with an anger in her eyes that is more than any seven-year-old should have. "What difference does it make?"

She's right. What does it matter if anyone knows she's not a baby? It's just a matter of time before they figure all of us out anyway.

I reach down my shirt and take out the twenties. I give one to June. "Stay close by, though. I'm supposed to be watching you."

"Whoa." She looks at the money. "I can play a million games. Thanks." June spins around so fast her little dress flairs out.

I like making June happy. She's so mad most of the time that she hardly notices little things. A twenty-dollar bill is big enough to get her attention.

"I saw what you done."

My head snaps around at the sound of the voice.

Calvin's face hovers a foot over my head. His eyes are intense and serious, just like his dad Paul Ray's are when he's telling us a story he thinks we're going to learn from. Something about that look makes me feel good. I'm mostly invisible, but with him looking at me like that, I feel seen. Calvin is half smiling and holding onto the hem of his shirt like he's about to lift it up. I kind of wish he would, but at the same time I hope he doesn't.

A weird feeling grabs my stomach, like the knot from before came untied.

His smile flashes in his eyes. He looks happy, excited, like a kid on his birthday who's just been handed a package. I catch a whiff of soap and that slight doggy smell that lingers in his bedroom. It smells good enough that I'm tempted to step a little closer to him.

"I saw what you done." He tilts his chin at the twenty I've still got in my hand.

I fold the money in half and stuff it in my pocket a little too fast. I feel off balance, like I'm getting caught in a lie. Something I *never* do. "There's nothing to tell," I say. My voice wavers. I sound like a liar. Pits!

"Saw you do it. Saw you reach in that guy's pocket."

I'm pretty sure I'm going to puke. How I'm feeling on the inside must show on my face.

"Don't worry." He puts his hand on my shoulder. "I'm not going to tell."

My instinct is to shake his hand off. I stop myself because that will make me look even guiltier. His big fingers grab onto me, not tight but not too loose either. The pukey feeling shifts into something different. Kind of like the feeling when a roller coaster is tick, tick, ticking up the track. Is he telling the truth? Will he really not tell even though his dad is the sheriff? His grin grows wider and shinier somehow. "You want to get a Coke or something?" he asks really nice, like he cares if I say yes or no.

"I don't know," I say.

His hand grows heavier. It's slightly damp. I want to go with him, I think I do, but I've never met someone from outside my family who knows so much about me. I like that he knows, but also I don't like it. It's exciting and scary at the same time. I guess I believe him. What other choice do I have?

I glance over at June. She's convinced someone to lift her up on a stool and she's leaning over the counter of the ring toss. She's going to win something. The carny will take all her money, but he won't let her leave without a prize. She's too cute and too small. And hopefully she remembers a thing or two about the power of little girl tears.

"Come on." Calvin's hand is still on my shoulder. "I'm buying." His voice is deeper than other boys'. It's a rumbling voice, but soft and slow too, because he's from Oklahoma. Maybe he's not exactly a boy. But he's Paul Ray's son, so he can't be a man. I decide he must be something in between.

The way he says he's buying like we're going to the bar at the racetrack makes me feel grown up. I'm not beautiful like my mom or pretty like Lainey, but when he says that, I feel like I am.

We walk over to the concession stand and the hand he has on me slides easily down and we're walking together with his arm around me like we're boyfriend and girlfriend. It's weird but nice. The soapy, doggy smell is all around me like a blanket.

There are two girls I recognize from school up at the counter ahead of us. When they turn around, big sodas and chocolate-covered pretzels in their hands, they look surprised to see us behind them. They look afraid, actually, but that doesn't make sense. One of them, the girl with the slightly blonder hair—Gayla or Gay Anne—opens her mouth to say something to me, which she has never done before.

"Go on. Get along," Calvin says to her before she has a chance to speak.

The girl looks like she might cry.

Her friend, Maitlin or Caitlin, bumps her hard. "Go, go!"

The first girl looks me hard in the eyes, like she's trying to tell me something, then both of them run away.

What is their problem? Townies are so odd.

Calvin gives me a big paper cup filled with the good kind of slushy ice and some sort of reddish liquid. "I got you a Suicide."

"What's that?" I wonder if this is another one of those things that everybody but me knows.

"You'll like it. It's all the flavors in one cup. Drink it down a little so I can put in the good stuff."

I take a big drink. It's extra sweet and tastes mostly like Dr. Pepper. It's not my favorite, but it's okay. Brain freeze tickles around the top of my head but doesn't take hold.

We drift away from the concession stand.

Calvin takes a silver flask out of his back pocket. He rests his cup on a ledge while he unscrews the top and pours clear liquid into his cup.

"Give it here." He indicates my cup and holds the flask out to me.

"What is it?"

"Part of the Suicide."

I know what it is. I've been around enough to know liquor when I see it. I'm not sure why I asked. Something to say, I guess. I always did want to try drinking. I hold out my cup.

He fills up my cup to the rim. "Stir it up real good." He grabs my straw and swishes it around. "If you stir it up, it don't taste so bad."

I take a taste. It's kind of like gasoline with a little sweetness mixed in, but I pretend I like it anyway. This makes Calvin happier than it seems like it should. He's standing still, but his body is moving in the way a puppy's does when it's trying hard to hold its energy in.

Baby June has moved on from the ring toss. She's shooting rubber balls from an air gun at crazy-looking clown heads. She did okay at the last game. She's got a stuffed donkey sitting at her feet.

"I've got to go check on my sister."

"You coming back?" There's a tremble in his voice like he really and truly wants me to say yes.

I shrug out from under his arm as though I just might have somewhere better to be; but before I can take even one step toward my sister, Paul Ray, dressed up in his sheriff's uniform, steps up to the game June is playing and snatches her up. Baby June squeals and kicks. "I was winning, motherfucker!"

I glance over at Calvin. He's ducked out of sight around the side of a tent. He holds his finger up to let me know he doesn't want me to say anything about him to his dad.

Paul Ray clamps his hand over June's mouth, which doesn't do a thing to settle her down. The opposite, in fact.

Paul Ray doesn't quite get Baby June. He treats her like she's a baby even though he's heard her talk and seen her walk like herself. He seems to be holding two truths in his head at the same time. Can people even do that?

"Jessup, what's your sister doing out here by her lone self?" He raises his voice to be heard over the drone of the music, the bubble of the crowd and the calls of the carnies.

"I'm watching her, Paul Ray," I call back. I don't rush over to them. I probably should, but I don't. I cast my eyes sideways. Calvin is still squatting down beside the tent with his finger to his lips. Something is weird in his eyes. He's scared of something.

Paul Ray hitches June up on his shoulder and takes several strides toward me. "Don't look like it to me." He's trying to sound gruff and mean, but it isn't working. I like Paul Ray's big face, with the mustache as prickly as a toothbrush. And his wide, happy smile that makes me feel the way eating eggs sunny side up with crispy bacon does on cold mornings when all the windows are frosty.

June is still kicking and squirming, but not so hard anymore.

Calvin hunkers down like he's trying to make himself invisible.

"Where's your mama, anyhow?" Paul Ray asks.

Pits, pits, pits. What am I supposed to say to that? My mind races to find a good answer. He doesn't know? Nobody called him to take my mom to jail yet.

"She's with Lainey," I say. That's the truth. The absolute truth.

That seems good enough for Paul Ray, which is something I didn't expect.

"I'm going to take this girl on home. Past her bedtime. You coming?"

My insides knot up. I take a big drink of my Suicide. This time it tastes more like gasoline mixed with cherry coke. I don't feel anything. I already know what I'm going to say, so why do I have this feeling like I'm standing on the high dive at the pool at the Howard Johnson's? I know I'm going to jump, but if I want to I can still climb back down the ladder.

"I'm going to stay for a while," I say. "If that's okay," I add, just to show him the respect he's due.

June's eyes are as mad as I've ever seen them. "Don't you leave me." Tears dribble down her face. She hardly ever cries. Never did, even when she really was a baby. "Don't you leave me."

Paul Ray scrunches his mustache over to one side like he's thinking it over. "Alrighty, can't see no harm in you staying a while. You got some money?" He props June on his shoulder and grabs his wallet with his other hand. He holds it open. "Get you one of them twenties."

I almost say no, because nobody should be that nice to a shadow like me. I would have stolen that twenty and more if opportunity had ever presented itself.

"Thanks," I say. I feel like maybe I might cry too. I can't figure out why.

Paul Ray turns away and lumbers toward the parking lot.

June looks over his shoulder at me. "Don't leave me. Dontleavemedonleavemedonleaveme." Her words blur together and become a single sound like a train blowing its horn as it passes out of town.

Baby June will understand one day. How am I supposed to take care of a kid like her? She'll be better off with someone who isn't a shadow.

I tuck Paul Ray's money into my pocket with the other twenty I stashed there. I catch a glimpse of Gayla or Gay Anne walking fast toward the parking lot. She's with a woman who's every bit as blond as she is. Her mother. Has to be. The mother whips her head from side to side like she's a mouse with a cat on her tail. She breaks into a full run, dragging her daughter with her, when she spies Paul Ray.

I walk back over to where Calvin is beside the tent. He's on his feet.

"Why were you hiding from your dad?"

"Me and him don't get along."

"Oh." Paul Ray seems easy enough to get along with, but what do I know? Maybe he's different with his own kids.

"You want to ride the Ferris wheel?"

I turn my head up to look. Red and yellow lights wink in the blue velvet sky. A big full moon makes the night brighter than it needs to be. At the top, three seniors I recognize from school are rocking their basket. One boy with a red rash of pimples across his nose is doing the rocking. The other has his arms around a curvy red-haired girl who's pretending to be afraid. The top of the Ferris wheel looks like it would be a great place to be, but I can't picture myself up there. It's not a place a shadow would go.

"Do you think we could walk around a while first?"

"I guess. If that's what you want to do." He reaches out and grabs my hand. He's trembling a little, which makes me feel powerful. I've never made anyone nervous before.

We embark on our stroll down the midway. The salty oil of popcorn, the sticky pink of cotton candy, and the corny sweet of hushpuppies mingle in a cloud of carnival perfume.

"You want another drink?" Calvin asks, making his cup gurgle. We've walked to the edge of the midway, almost to where the mesquite scrub and brambles start.

"No thanks."

"You want me to make that one stronger?"

The alcohol doesn't seem to be doing anything, and I'd like to know what all the fuss is about. "Okay."

He tosses his empty out into the dark tangle just beyond where we're standing and takes my cup from me. He pours more liquor from his flask into my cup, and then takes a swig. As he swishes my cup around to mix things up, I let my eyes wander out into the field. I try as hard as I can to remember exactly what I saw on that very first night we got to Frederick.

"You want to walk back?" he asks.

"Let's walk around the edge instead."

Calvin's smile looks just like that bacon-and-egg smile of his dad's. He wraps his hands around my arms and pulls me up against him. He leans down and presses his mouth against mine. He pushes his tongue in my mouth.

I'm still holding my cup, and the sweaty wax paper is squishing up against him. I'm not sure what to do with my other hand, so I let it settle on his hip. He feels hard. Muscle hard, so different from anyone I've ever touched before. His tongue is in my mouth and I wonder what he thinks of my teeth. No one has ever been on the inside of my mouth before. Not even my mom.

"I like you," he says in a gasping-for-air breathy voice.

I like him too, but I'm not so sure I like kissing. I know better than to say that. I like that he wants to kiss me even if I'm not all that thrilled with the actual activity. Maybe I'll get used to it. Having another person's tongue in my mouth is the weirdest thing I've ever experienced. "Umm hmmm," I murmur.

When it's over and he pulls back, I'm relieved.

"Let's walk some more," I say. I take his hand and squeeze it.

"Awright," he says. "You want to go somewhere? You know, more private."

I nod like that's exactly the thing I want most. I've got a pretty good idea what he's got on his mind, but I'm absolutely sure I don't have the first clue about how to do what he wants. He's going to think I'm really stupid. I wish I was more sexy.

As we're walking around the outside edge, I look for the white shell of our camper. I know it's not far away. Calvin drapes his arm around my shoulder and lets his hand rest on my boob. Not that it's much of a boob, but it's all I've got. It feels weird when he rubs his pinky finger over my nipple. It's like he doesn't even notice I'm only wearing a training bra instead of a real one.

"Do you know I sleep in your bed?" I say. My voice sounds kind of gravelly. I wanted it to sound grown up and sexy, but instead it sounds like I need to clear my throat.

"Yup. I knew that."

"Did your dad tell you?"

"Me and him don't talk."

The music from the carnival sounds far away, like the sound has traveled across a lake. A pump jack thump-thumps in the distance. I can't see it, cranking around and around pulling the oil from the ground, but I hear it louder than my own heartbeat. Seems odd Calvin doesn't talk to his own father, the person he's spent all his life with. How could he possibly know what goes on in the house if his dad didn't say?

Calvin pulls me in closer against his body. Walking feels a little awkward. We aren't exactly in sync as we wind our way through the trailers at the edge of the carnival. I still like having his arm around me, even though it would be easier to walk without it. Nobody's around. The carnival seems to be winding down for the night. Sometimes we step out into the overgrowth until it gets too thick and we tromp through the plant life and back onto the blacktop. I still haven't spotted the camper, but we're close. We must be.

"Why don't you talk to your dad?" I ask.

"He don't like some of the things I done. He says they ain't right and I can't be his son unless I change my ways."

"What kind of things?"

"Don't matter. Ain't like nothing is gonna change. I'm different from other folks. There's nothing I can do about it." He flips his long brown hair over his collar. It falls on his shoulder in a nice soft-looking way.

I have the urge to pet it.

"It's just how I am."

"I know exactly what you mean," I say. I get an excited feeling. I *do* know exactly what he means. I've never met anyone outside of my family who was an outsider like us. Pity wells up in my chest. I think it might choke me. It must be even harder to be different without even one other person to understand.

I understand him, though.

"You want to be my girlfriend?"

I never thought I wanted a boyfriend before. My mom has them all the time and it never works out all that good, but for some reason this seems like a good idea. Like something I could be better at than my mom.

"Yeah." I feel like I know Calvin better than anyone. It's like there's a new member of my family. I can tell him anything. Everything. I don't know where to start.

We stop walking again, and Calvin leans down. I get the feeling he's going to kiss me again, but he doesn't. He puts his hands on my head and tangles his fingers in my hair. He's holding onto my hair kind of tight, but it doesn't hurt. Not really.

"Can I lop off a piece of your hair?"

"For your box?" The words spill out before I even think about them.

Calvin's eyes flash, and all the muscles in his face tighten up. "What box is that?"

It's probably private. Guilt churns in my stomach. I shouldn't have looked at Calvin's personal stuff.

With one hand he grips my hair; with the other he reaches into his pocket and pulls out a folding knife. He flicks it open with his thumb.

The way he's holding my hair makes my head tilt to the side. Everything looks just a little off-kilter from this perspective. The back of the Ace Hardware looks exactly the same as the first night I saw it.

It must be pretty late by now. The doctor has probably figured out that Lainey's leg isn't broken, and my mom is probably on the way to jail in the back of Paul Ray's sheriff car.

The pump jack thump thumps, only this time my heart is thumping louder.

"I'm just going to cut off a little chunk. Only because I like you so much."

"Okay," I say, but it doesn't feel like it's okay. I'm not so worried about what I want to tell Calvin anymore. He doesn't seem in the mood to hear about me. I shouldn't have listened to my mom and practiced my feminine wiles. I think I might have used too much.

I remember that one complete fingernail, not a clipping, that Calvin keeps in that box. How would someone come by something like that?

Calvin holds my hair so tight tears are welling in my eyes. He saws with his knife. It's a relief when he cuts through and my head is free again. I'm tempted to touch my hair and see how much is gone. I'm feeling mad about this now that it's sunk in some, but this isn't the type of situation where getting mad is going to do any good. He did it because he likes me, after all. Even if it is a messed up thing to do. Pits. This is not going how I thought it would.

Calvin wraps his arms around me and pushes his mouth against mine. His tongue feels like a big chunk of meat. I want to breathe more than I can with him on me like this. His leg keeps wrapping around me like he's trying to knock me down. I don't want to fall. Not now. Not here on the blacktop behind the dirty carnival vans.

The top of the camper, the part that fits over the cab where me, Lainey, and June watch what goes on after my mom sends us to bed, peeks out from a tangle of trees not much taller than me. I feel like I just saw Thanksgiving dinner laid out in all its glory. That camper is the best home I ever had. Our old pickup might have a flat tire or even two and probably not too much gas, but I know exactly where the screwdriver is that starts the ignition. I can make it go. I'm sure of it. I can get that old truck out of this field and out of Frederick. I bet the forty dollars I've got will get me most of the way to Dallas. In a flash the memory comes back to me that I never gave my mom the take. I've got plenty of money. I can go anywhere.

"Wait," I say, pushing Calvin away and untangling myself from his octopus grip. "I got a better idea."

"What's that?"

Before he even gets out the whole question, I leap away and plow into the overgrown field. I crash through the weeds and branches. I don't even care how bad I'm getting scratched. Now I'm the mouse with a cat on my tail. I've just got to get to the camper.

Breathless, I finally make it. I jerk open the door. The smell of my mom's Opium perfume and the liniment we rub on Baby June's knees splashes in my face. I glance back.

"You got a camper?" Calvin grins and stomps down a bunch of weeds. He reaches out for me.

As hard as I'd run, I only managed to keep two steps ahead of him. I dive for the screwdriver, but he grabs me around the waist and lifts me up before I can get it.

Now I know how Baby June feels when people pick her up. I kick and thrash, but it doesn't do any good. I scream, and he clamps his hand over my mouth.

I can't get enough air in. I can barely hear the thump-thump of the pump jack over the sound of my heart. I can barely hear the whoop-whoop of the sheriff's siren.

Calvin opens the door to the camper and lugs me inside. He drops me on the floor and falls on top of me.

I wriggle and writhe but can't get out from under him. The button on my shirt tears off. He's heavy on my chest and his hand is clamped down hard on my mouth. The air won't come no matter how hard I try to get it.

"Hey, look!" I say, gasping. "It's a good one. Heads up."

Maybe it's my words or maybe it's the whoop-whoop of the sheriff's siren and the crunch of men pushing through the mesquite brush that catches his attention and makes him look up.

It's too late for us. We're always going to be different, and they're coming to lock us up.

I push and scramble just enough. I lunge for the penny. My shadow spreads out before me, long and lanky as a willow. My hand wraps around the copper. I melt into its warm chocolaty embrace.

As the siren whoops grow insistent and the sheriff's men shout to each other how they found the camper, poor Calvin finds himself holding what's left of the girl I used to be like a scarecrow husk.

It's a trick, but a good one. Or maybe it's not.

I am a shadow.

A Thousand Stitches

"It was not only pathetic, it was ludicrous," a writer, whose name I forget, said about his father's tailor shop.

That's a pretty apt description of the situation in the back room at Malley's Dry Cleaners. I'm not going to be here much longer, which is a good thing, because I'd be forced to take desperate measures if this situation wasn't temporary. I'm just working until I save up enough to move to New York.

Judy says we used to get all different kinds of work. She says we even used to get orders to make suits and evening gowns. That would be so sweet. I would love to design and make something like that. I'd love to have a job where I could use my talent. Why someone would go to a tailor shop in the back room at Malley's Cleaners to get their evening gown made, I don't know, but that's what Judy says. Since I've been here, what we mostly get is wedding dresses. Sometimes we replace a zipper or put new buttons on a dress shirt, but the vast majority of the work is taking the feathers, sequins, or jewels off the wedding gowns so they can be cleaned, then sewing all the stuff back on once they're done. Even though there are a million colors in the world, every single one of the princess bridal dresses are white. We have a whole separate rack just for white thread. The women in this town don't have a speck of imagination. Nobody here does. I can't wait to leave. My wedding dress, not that I'd ever want one, but if I did, my dress would be hurricane-sky yellow or pumpkin orange. Something that shows that I'm not just another cow in the herd. Judy says hers was ruby red. I guess Judy was married once. I have trouble imagining that.

Even after they've been cleaned, the wedding dresses smell faintly of the expensive perfume the bride bought for her special day and never wore again. A surprising number of them have the lingering scent of vomit and sex. "Special day" smells, I guess. The work is the essence of meaningless. These dresses will be stashed away in attics or cedar trunks, never to be worn again. I feel like I'm sewing up shrouds, except my work doesn't even get to clothe a corpse. It just gets buried.

I remove the last of the seed pearls from a bodice and place them in a baby food jar. I sit cross-legged on my bench because that's how tailors are supposed to sit. Judy says it's going to twist my spine and make me a cripple before I'm forty. Judy always says things like that. I'm not exactly sure where she gets her information. And even if it is true, forty is a long way away. I'll probably never even make it that far. My mom doesn't think I'll make it to middle age. She thinks I need to change my ways. She might be right.

I like doing things the traditional way. It makes me feel authentic. Sewing is the only real thing left. Writers write on computers and singers' voices are auto-tuned. Movies are full of fake special effects. Even photographers manipulate images so much that they don't have anything to do with what the eye actually sees. Sewing is the only real thing left. There's no way to do it electronically. It's honest and true. That's a good thing.

A wisp of menthol smoke wafts out of the ladies' room that only Judy and I use. The water runs a really long time, then the door under the sink slams shut. I'm pretty sure Judy stashed her pillow and comforter under there. The hiss of hair spray from a can filters through the hum of dry cleaning machines and the mechanical rumble of the overhead racks in the rest of the store. She's been in there for several hours, ever since I got to work this morning. Judy has been pushing the boundaries for months, staying in the ladies' room longer each day. No one has noticed yet, or maybe they look the other way because she's worked here so long. I don't mind. Sometimes I work extra fast so she won't have to work so hard to catch up. Not that she would. She covers for me, too, when I need a nap.

The dresses we are working on fill the racks that mark the boundaries of our little enclosure, like puffy, bloated dancers in a chorus line. Something about the way air circulates through Malley's makes the fabric swish ever so slightly, as if someone on the other side has brushed their hand along them. It's creepy when we come in early or stay late and no one else is in the building. It's creepy all the time, actually.

Judy's cigarette hits the water in the toilet with a satisfying sizzle. She steps out of the ladies' room with every loop and wave of her silver hair in exactly the right spot. Her lipstick is perfect. It doesn't bleed into the creases around her lips like I've seen on some old ladies. I wish I had the confidence to wear the shades of red she does. She smoothes her leopard-print dress over her angular hips and pushes her ruffled cuffs up to her elbows as she sits in her chair in front of the dusty old treadle machine that hasn't been used for as long as I've been here. Judy's eyes look puffy. Her skin seems a little gray under her makeup. I hope she's not sick. She'd never admit it if she was.

"He's going to catch you smoking," I say.

Judy pulls an enormous mound of crinoline and white silk onto her lap. For a moment it seems as if it might swallow her, but with a no-nonsense air she pushes the glasses hanging around her neck up on her nose and crushes the unruly dress into submission.

"The old man didn't care if we smoke. Why should he?" She punctuates her words with a jab of the tiny golden scissors she uses to snip especially tight stitches.

I shrug. "He's an idiot."

"Now there's an understatement. That brat better watch his step around me, or I'll bring the old man back from the other side to give him a stern 'how do you do.'" Judy's laugh is as raspy as a fine-tooth saw and always seems about to decay into a fit of coughing. It exactly captures her sense of humor: harsh, and always in danger of becoming something more sinister. That's a good thing. More people should laugh in a dangerous way.

"Can you do that?" I tag the dress I was working on and put it in the bin for the tumblers. "Can you bring him back? You know, summon him?" I'm not sure if I believe in ghosts, but it would be absolutely perfect if they were real. I'll believe it when I see it.

"I've never tried." Judy's scissors make little *tic, tic, tic* sounds as she removes stitches. "But if anyone could raise that man from the dead, I'd be the one who could do it." Judy winks at me to make sure I don't miss the double entendre.

The dresses sway. The petticoats rustle. The hairs on my arms prickle as a gust of cold air blows over me.

I glance up at the vent. The red ribbon is waving like a semaphore flag.

I let my mouth fall open in mock surprise. "You had an affair with the boss."

"The idea that he was the boss might not stand up to scrutiny." Judy laughed her dangerous laugh.

"But he was married."

"Minor detail."

Judy is so completely awesome. I hope I have a life like hers. I will, I know it, once I get to New York.

"Does Ron know?"

"Does Ron know what?" Ron pushes a clothing cart piled high with garments through a gap between the racks of swaying dresses.

I snap my mouth shut and wait for my heart to stop pounding. I hate when Ron sneaks up on us.

"Is that the same dress you've been working on for the last three days?" He glares at the pile of silk and crinoline piled on the treadle machine.

Judy looks over the top of her glasses. If she had laser vision, she would have burned a hole right through the spot where Ron's too-narrow tie knots around his over-long neck.

"Did you not get my email?"

Ron smells faintly of lighter fluid mixed with rotten banana. It's from the dipropylene glycol he used to replace the perchloroethylene his father preferred. To be fair, perc's not a good cleaning solvent. It was the first carcinogen ever identified by the CDC. But this new stuff has to be even worse. Ron worries about fire hazards constantly. It's a good thing, since the new chemical is probably as flammable as it smells. By the strength of his pungent aroma, it would seem like he climbs right in the machines and tumbles around with the clothes. He's a hands-on kind of guy. Not that that's so commendable in a work-ethic sort of way. He just thinks everyone else is too stupid to do things right.

"Well?"

"I don't have email," I say. I'm supposed to get email on my phone and tell Judy, but I never remember to charge it. I'm not really into electronic communication anyway.

"I thought we solved this," Ron says. He's trying to hold his body like he's in charge. Maybe he read a self-help book about body language. The effect is comic, like *Othello* performed in extra-amateur community theater. It's clear that even though he's trying not to show it, he's intimidated by Judy.

Judy releases the dress, and its crinolines expand and swallow up the treadle machine.

"Why aren't these garments logged?" Ron grips the handle of the cart and draws his lips into a thin line. He speaks in what I can tell he intends to be a forceful tone.

Even though Judy's stooped over a little because she's old, she's easily four inches taller than Ron. That can't help his body language any. She jiggles the cord on the hotplate. It crackles a little and she places the kettle on it.

"You can't have that back here." His voice wavers, like he had to gather his courage to speak at all as he points at the hotplate. He looks at me like I'm the one making tea.

"The old man authorized it back when you were in grade school."

"Get rid of it." Ron's neck and cheeks turn red. "Today."

Judy folds her arms and steps between Ron and the hot plate. "We'll just have to take it up with the old man, won't we?"

Ron clenches his teeth like he's forcing himself to stay calm. In the midst of the racks of rainbow-hued spools of thread, baskets of fabric scraps, teetering boxes, jars of buttons, and bags stuffed with spare doodads and dangles, as Judy calls them, he looks drained of all color like a pencil sketch. Ron is out of his element in our exploded Barbie Dreamhouse that robins have made into a nest. As crowded and cluttered as it is, I like our little work space. It may look like a mess, but we can find things. My studio in New York, when I get one, is going to be just like this, only bigger.

"Why aren't you doing your work? We've got people waiting."

"I am," I say, waving my hand at the racks of wedding dresses. If we ever run out of work from the racks, there's a teetering stack of fancy dress store boxes stuffed with even more.

"Not the bridals, Laura Beatty." Ron's voice squeaks with the intensity of his emotion. "You have to read your email."

Everyone calls me by my first and last name, like it's one word. I can't even remember when it started. I used to hate it, but I don't anymore. I'm like the opposite of Beyoncé.

"Well, what then? I don't know what you want."

Ron's sigh is as loud as the explosion of steam from the presser. "The tailor shop needs to start pulling its weight. It needs to generate more business."

"People don't tailor their clothes the way they used to do." Judy touches the tea kettle to see if it's hot. It must not be yet. Some tea would be nice. It would also be nice if Ron would go back to whatever he was doing before.

"New policy." Ron folds his arms just like Judy. He sets his jaw. He's thought about how he's going to say this. He probably practiced in the mirror. "Zippers, buttons, and hems, same-day service."

"What!" Judy's eyes flash with anger. She stomps her foot. "That's as idiotic as you are."

"You're already behind." Ron shoves the cart in my direction as though he didn't even hear Judy call him idiotic. "Focus. This has to be done by 5pm."

"Or what?" Judy's question is more of a threat.

"All this?" I stare at the mountain of jeans with pink ribbons threaded through their button holes to mark broken zippers, slacks and skirts pinned up with green-headed pins, and shirts with yellow flags safety-pinned where they need a button. "This is too much for one day."

"One basket equals one day's pay." Ron's smug little eyes narrow to self-satisfied slits.

"You can do that," I say, but a tremble works its way up from my hands to my face because I don't have any power. None at all. Without this job I'll never make it to New York. I should never have bought those new winter boots. Or other things that I'm not going to beat myself up about. Everybody messes up sometimes. My savings are even close to where they should be.

The tea kettle vibrates on the hotplate as the water begins to boil. "You can't pay sweatshop wages," Judy says. "Not in this day and age."

"That's right." Tears feel like they're about to roll down my cheeks. This is not the time for tears. "It's illegal."

Ron's smug little smirk grows into a full-blown grin. "Have your law-yer call me." He tries to hold my gaze like he's tough, but he looks away first. To hide his failure, he pushes aside the poof of the wedding dresses and marches down the aisle in the direction of the front counter.

"That little weasel." Judy takes two teacups and a tin of Earl Gray from the shelf. "Don't worry about him."

I frantically paw through the basket of work. "There's more here than we can do in two days. Even if we work faster than we ever have before, there's no way we can get it done." I jerk open the drawer where we keep the zippers and dig through them, looking for a match. "What if we have to order supplies?" Panic is rising up in me and squeezing my throat closed. I'm more aware than ever before of the toxic dry-cleaning fumes. I want to go outside to breathe some regular air, but I don't have time.

"A thousand stitches, right?" I try to smile at Judy, but my face feels twitchy and wrong. I grab the button tin. It slips from my hands. Buttons scatter, bouncing and rolling in every direction. I fall to my knees.

"Leave that." Judy says, holding out a teacup. "Sit."

"But..."

"Sit."

I take the tea and sit on my tailor's bench. My mind races as it enumerates all the little tasks that fill the basket. "He can't get away with this."

"He'll get away with it," Judy says, "over my dead body."

I don't know where she gets her confidence, but she says it with such conviction I almost believe her.

"Drink up."

I take a sip of the tea. I don't really like it. It tastes more flowery than ordinary tea, because the tin has been stored next to the perfume-soaked wedding gowns for so long. The essence of long-gone and stored away "special days" floats like a skin of grease on my tea.

"Drink it down."

I take another sip.

"All of it." Judy watches as I drain my cup. She takes it from me and tips the tea leaves into the saucer.

Her chair squeals as she slides it across the floor and wedges it next to my bench. She peers over the tops of her glasses as she studies the leaves. "Uh-huh. Just what I thought." She puts the saucer under my nose. "See that?"

I see a bunch of soggy tea leaves that smell even more sickly than they did in my cup. "I guess."

The whites of Judy's eyeballs have a yellowish tinge. Maybe it's because she's tired. Her breath smells odd too, like spoiled fruit.

"Then it's settled." Judy places the saucer on the edge of my bench.

"What is?"

"You're going to New York."

"Is that what the tea leaves said?" I start to feel a little better, like maybe there's a glimmer of hope after all. "I've been so worried I won't have enough—"

Judy grabs her big purse with all of the pockets and drags it onto her lap. She digs around inside. She frowns as if she can't find what she's looking for. "I remember now. It's in the drawer." She points.

I squat down to inspect the contents of the drawer. It's where we keep our invoices and order forms. I riffle through the paperwork.

"There. That's it."

I pull out a manila envelope closed with a rubber band.

"What is it?"

"Open it."

I unwind the elastic and reach my hand inside. Money. A lot of it. "What—"

"You're going to New York." Judy stands up fast, like she's in a hurry to be somewhere. "Today." She grabs the corner of the sewing machine table to steady herself. "That's three thousand dollars. Enough to get you started. This is your chance."

Why is she doing this? Judy won't even loan me a dollar for a soda. She is the definition of tight with a dollar.

"I can't take this," I say, but I know I can. She wouldn't offer it to me if she didn't want me to take it. With this much money, I can pay all the incidental fees that my student loan doesn't cover. I can find a place to live. I can be enrolled in Parsons by the spring semester.

Judy doesn't bother to argue with me. She knows I'm going. She knows I want this more than anything ever.

"You can take that money, all of it. No strings attached except one."

I clutch the envelope a little tighter than is probably polite.

"You have to go now."

I blink at her. "You mean right now? This minute?"

"Yes."

I open my mouth to argue, but I don't. There is no reason not to walk outside and take the bus to the train station. Not one single reason. I'm really going. Today.

"You're going to do fine. Remember, it takes a thousand stitches to make one dollar. Don't waste any more stitches. You use yours to make the prettiest dresses New York has ever seen."

"Why don't you come with—"

"You'll need a winter coat." Judy grabs her nubby wool jacket with the real fox collar off the hanger. She drapes it around my shoulders. "Make me proud of you, Laura Beatty."

Judy never says she expects me to fail. She's seen me screw up just like everybody else has, but she never tells me I drink too much or I stay out too late and take crazy chances. She always talks to me like the things I dream are already real. How am I going to leave her behind?

"What are you going to do?" I ask. I wish I wasn't crying, but there's nothing I can do to stop it.

Judy smiles a smile that's as dangerous as her laugh. "I'm going to take a nap." She turns away, kicks off her shoes in the middle of the floor, and walks into the ladies' room. The door closes with a delicate click. I breathe in the stale perfume and chemical smell of Malley's one last time. The scent of menthol cigarettes drifts from under the ladies' room door.

*   *   *

My bus pulls into Port Authority at 5 a.m. This is the time I get up most days so I can get to Malley's by six. This time of year it's dark this early. Not here, though. More than a half an hour ago the lights of Manhattan had changed the velvet black tapestry of the night sky to the color of neon dusk.

My heart races as I step off the train and into the river of early commuters. I think about pinching myself. I am here. Against all the odds, I am here.

The ring of an old-fashioned telephone startles me. I guess I remembered to charge it for once. I reach into my pocket and pull it out. "Hello."

"Laura Beatty, oh my God. I've been so worried."

"What's wrong, Mom?"

"I've been calling you for hours. Why haven't you answered your phone? I've been worried sick." Her voice was shaky, like when I was a kid and she found me at the bottom of the stairs with a broken arm. Or later, that one time after that party that didn't end well. Her voice sounds far away, even farther away than it really is, like I'm talking to her through a portal to a different time.

"I'm fine. Why wouldn't I be?"

"There was a fire at Malley's. The whole place burned, burned to the ground. Nobody knew where you were."

"Oh no. Was anyone hurt?"

I can't believe that Malley's is gone. Now I don't even have the option to fail. I don't have anywhere to go back to.

"Everyone got out in time, except no one could find you."

"I'm here. I'm fine."

I let the flow of the crowd push me onto 42nd St.

"Where's Judy? Did she get out in time?"

"Not that again, Laura Beatty." My mom sighs like she's caught me stealing from her liquor cabinet again. "I thought we decided when we met with the doctor that it isn't healthy to talk about these things as though they were real."

My mother has no idea, no idea, what's real or what's not. By "these things" she means delusions I do not have. The doctor was her idea. Judy says you can learn a lot about what's wrong with a person by watching what they try to make other people do. My mom would be a lot better off if she'd just admit she's the one with the problem. She's totally without spirituality.

"Okay, Mom. But no one was hurt, right?"

"That's right." My mom pauses to inhale. I can tell she's gathering steam for a lecture.

"I've got to go, Mom. I love you," I say to prevent myself from placing yet another wedge between my mother and me.

"Where are you, anyway?"

"New York," I say, and click my phone shut before I can hear her full exclamation of shock and dismay. My mom doesn't think I can handle New York. I've screwed up a few things in the past. She doesn't have a lot of faith in me.

As I slide my phone back into the pocket of Judy's coat, my fingers graze against something. I pull out an elegant golden cigarette case. I snap it open and take out a slim menthol cigarette. As I pause to light it, I catch a glimpse of myself in a window. I look like a woman who knows what she wants and who's sure of where she's going. I breathe in the smoke and let the essence of Judy swirl around in me. I flick my ashes on the sidewalk. Judy's ruby-red lipstick stains the filter of my cigarette. I like that.

Effigy

Tiny white lights looped off the trellis surrounding the patio of Sampang Café and reflected off the tops of the glass tables. For just an instant Gwen felt off balance, as though she were supposed to remember how to pick out a meaningful constellation from the sea of artificial stars. Someone told her once, or maybe she read it somewhere, that the constellations helped ancient people remember their history. That seemed unlikely. There was no meaning in the stars, not even the real ones. Why should she even try to remember that stuff? It was hard enough to remember how to navigate the city.

"Gwen?" a man called out.

Gwen hurried toward his table, then remembered to slow down so she wouldn't draw attention to the fact she was fifteen minutes late. He wouldn't notice unless she made a big deal of it.

Probably.

It wasn't her fault. She'd left her phone on top of a stack of boxes in her apartment. Without it, it had been a nightmare finding the Culver City restaurant. Luckily, she'd written the address on a scrap of paper. Most people would have given up, but Gwen didn't have that option.

The air was heavy with the smells of curry and fish. Without being too obvious, Gwen peeked at what people were eating. She didn't recognize anything. She hoped Indonesians didn't eat fish bladders or chicken beaks. She should have researched that ahead of time, especially since she planned to land this job as a nanny. Living with the family, she'd surely have to partake of the cuisine.

Gwen smiled as the man stood up to shake her hand. Victor Sunjaya, *Soon-jai-ya*. He wasn't old or young; good-looking or ugly. He was exactly in-between. He was the same height as she was, five foot seven. She thought he'd be taller.

For a man who ran an import/export company, he didn't look especially distinguished.

She should keep an open mind. Judging people by their appearance was wrong. She was going to be his nanny, not his wife, so his looks didn't matter.

It was a little odd to meet for a job interview in a restaurant at night. A little odd, but not all that much. Not every Craigslist ad was posted by murderers and rapists. He was probably busy in the day importing and exporting, or maybe traveling to the company's main office in Jakarta. Once she was hired, she'd be travelling around the world in no time. Nannies got to do that.

"Did you find the place without trouble?" he asked as he sat down again, gesturing for her to do the same. He didn't have an accent, exactly, but there was something about the way he strung words together, *without trouble*, which seemed like it took effort. His teeth were remarkably white and straight.

Gwen smiled without showing hers. She couldn't remember if she'd brushed.

At the next table, a tall, dark-haired man with a fashionable haircut hissed at his wife. As if she were being purposefully defiant, she took her time letting her eyes wander back from Mr. Sunjaya and Gwen's table. The man said something in a language Gwen couldn't place. Indonesian, obviously. The woman narrowed her eyes at him and tucked a lock of her long expertly-coiffed hair behind her ear.

Gwen wished she'd gotten the nice haircut she'd wanted rather than the ten-dollar Supercut. She felt like a scarecrow compared to the woman at the next table. Saving the money didn't matter in the long run. She still came up short. First paycheck, she pledged to get her hair done properly.

"No problem at all, Mr. Sunjaya. Your directions were good, thank you." Gwen hoped he would say she should call him Victor, because his last name didn't exactly roll off her tongue. He didn't, but that would come later, once he got to know her better.

His eyes darted across the patio to the archway she'd just come through. They flitted back to her, then again to the archway, as if he were nervous or waiting for someone. That was probably where the waiters lingered, waiting for a sign from the guests. Maybe he was looking for a waiter, although the archway looked just like an exit to the parking lot.

"Would you like something, a coffee?" Mr. Sunjaya asked. "Waiter," he barked at a waiter who did not appear through the archway but looked up from a nearby table. Mr. Sunjaya's voice was surprisingly loud for such a small man. "Coffee."

The waiter nodded. He didn't seem at all annoyed that Mr. Sunjaya interrupted him. Victor must be an important person.

Gwen wasn't especially fond of coffee, but it was too late now. She'd drink it. It wasn't that big of a deal. When she was his nanny, she'd make hot chocolate for the child and always make extra for herself.

She reached into her bag and pulled out her résumé and slid it across the table. The thin white paper, not cream-colored and fabric-like, made her cringe. She'd spared no expense to get the very best résumés, only she'd forgotten to pick them up from the printer. Maybe it wouldn't matter. The type of résumé paper an applicant used wasn't that important.

Mr. Sunjaya took the paper from her. He seemed a bit distracted, like there was somewhere else he'd rather be. He glanced at it and set it down. He looked into Gwen's eyes. For just an instant she thought she saw a hint of something...sympathy, maybe...but it quickly passed.

His eyebrows were bushy with a few long stray gray hairs. He'd look ten years younger if he took care of that. Someday, when she was considered a member of the family, she'd mention it.

The waiter placed a miniature cup filled with ink-black liquid in front of her.

"Thank you," Gwen said.

Without asking, the waiter placed a delicate-looking glass in front of her and filled it with water from a pitcher.

"How old is your child?" Gwen asked. "Your daughter, right?"

Confusion flashed in Mr. Sunjaya's eyes for a second, but he quickly recovered. "Right, yes, my daughter." He glanced at the archway again.

The tiny lights climbed up one side and down the other. They were so much brighter than the stars in the sky, but just as meaningless. How could stars ever help anyone remember their history? There were so many. They were so random.

Gwen sipped her coffee. It tasted like someone had soaked cigarette butts in hot water. She resisted the urge to spit. That's not the kind of thing a nanny would do.

"Would you like to meet her?" Mr. Sunjaya pushed Gwen's résumé away without taking a second look at it.

"I have references if you'd like their numbers."

Mr. Sunjaya waved his hand to dismiss the idea. All the while, his eyes darted back and forth around the patio.

Gwen's stomach lurched. According to the notice the sheriff had pinned to the door of her apartment, at midnight tonight, in just a few hours, she was going to be locked out. She envied those people she ran into from time to time who could move home to Iowa or wherever when things got bad. How lucky they were to have the family home to run to when they needed to rebound from failure and nurse their humiliation. Those people acted like it was the worst that could happen. They were wrong.

"I'll bring her here." He slid back his chair and stood. "And you can meet her. You wait. Wait here until I return with my daughter and you will be her...*pengasuh*...babysitter."

"But...?" Gwen said. "Can I tell you about my experience with children?"

Gwen had none, but Mr. Sunjaya didn't need to know that. She had references that said she did. Gwen was going to love being a nanny. She never got to be a kid, not the way most kids did, with that thing that happened with her mother and her father nowhere to be found. When she was a nanny, she was going to play all the kid games and read all the kid books and eat all the kid food and be happy and safe and secure.

"I am giving to you the job," Mr. Sunjaya said without looking at Gwen. His eyes seemed to be focused on the tips of her fingers. "You should not try so hard."

"You are?" It felt like the sun bloomed inside her. A hundred questions flooded her head. She glanced at her résumé. What piece of information had secured the position for her? What did she say? What did she do? She couldn't even guess.

"I am going now." Mr. Sunjaya leaned toward her. Even though he was small for a man, he loomed over her. The mass of his body blocked the constellations of decorative light. Gwen tensed, and a flash of fear exploded in her chest as he reached down. This was an odd reaction to a man who had just given her a job. Mr. Sunjaya didn't put his hand on Gwen's shoulder as she thought he was going to do. He grabbed a box from the chair next to her and placed it on the table. "Please take care of my package while I am going to get my daughter."

"Okay." Gwen's voice rose at the end like she was asking a question. This was a perfectly normal request. He would bring the child back and then Gwen would be her nanny. It was perfect. It was the best possible outcome.

The box didn't take up much more room than a dinner plate. It was cardboard and looked like a shoebox, except the printing on the side wasn't English and a strip of silver duct tape sealed it. Someone had stabbed a few holes in the top with a sharp object, as though a small animal inside needed air.

Gwen poked the box. Nothing moved.

"No," Mr. Sunjaya said. There was a brittle edge to his voice. "Just watch it. Don't touch it for now."

Gwen peered at the box. She opened her mouth to ask a question, but Mr. Sunjaya cut her off.

He stepped back from the table. "I will go now."

"Okay," Gwen said.

"You will stay here with the package?"

"Yes." Gwen was surprised by a spike of annoyance. She made sure it didn't show on her face. She was going to be the best nanny ever. She would never get angry or forget to read a bedtime story.

"Do not leave the package here," he said.

"Okay." This time, even though she tried to prevent it, a little irritation crept into her tone. Did he think she was stupid? She knew how to keep an eye on a package.

He turned to the archway and walked as though he were in a hurry.

"Mr. Sunjaya?" Gwen called after him.

The people at the next table looked up. The man looked away and made a warning noise into his dinner plate. He said something that sounded a lot like *stay out of it*, but maybe he'd said something else entirely. The woman's eyes lingered on her a moment before she too turned back to her meal. She wore a pink cashmere cardigan just like the one Gwen had admired at Nordstrom's but hadn't had the money to buy.

Maybe she'd get that sweater with her first paycheck.

"Mr. Sunjaya," Gwen said again.

He turned.

"What is her name?"

Something terrifying happened behind Mr. Sunjaya's eyes. As though a shadow had fallen over him, his expression darkened. There was another emotion surging through him that Gwen couldn't quite identify, maybe confusion or dread.

"My daughter," he said. His words marched out of his mouth meticulously, as though he had to search for each one.

"I know. What's her name?" Gwen's voice was too loud. She wasn't the kind of person who yelled across rooms, let alone across restaurants. Most people learned that kind of thing from their mothers. Gwen had figured it out on her own.

The woman at the next table shifted her eyes to the side, gazing at her through a curtain of hair. The rope of pearls she wore nestled against the soft nap of her cardigan. She was casually elegant, as if she didn't know the value of the things she wore. Gwen wished she was more like her. She would be before long. First she'd be a nanny, then a personal assistant, then who knew?

Mr. Sunjaya held Gwen's gaze for a moment, then a moment longer. He forced the corners of his mouth into a smile that no one could pretend was genuine. He tilted his head at her as though he'd answered her question.

"I have given you the job."

Too quickly, at almost a run, he passed through the archway and disappeared from sight.

Gwen folded her hands in front of her at the table. The moments spooled out before her. She felt weird sitting alone in the restaurant. She felt as though her head had swollen to the size of a good carving pumpkin and was wobbling precariously on her shoulders. She couldn't catch anyone, but she could feel their eyes on her.

One after another, the diners finished their meals, pushed their plates away, paid their checks and drifted through the archway into the night. Gwen felt a little less uncomfortable as the people left.

Mr. Sunjaya's box sat on the table, taking up space like her dinner companion. Gwen entertained the idea of drawing a face on it with lipstick and engaging in conversation just to pass the time, but decided against acting so childish in public. A kid would appreciate something like that. She was going to be the best nanny ever.

The silver duct tape wasn't fully stuck down on one side. Gwen worried it with her fingernail. Someone before her had opened the box and resealed it. Mr. Sunjaya would never know if she looked inside. She hesitated. It would be just her luck that Mr. Sunjaya would return the moment she opened the box.

The waiter stopped at the edge of her table. He refilled her water glass. "Are you ready to order?" His hands trembled slightly as he held a pencil to a pad. He wouldn't look directly at her. Maybe it was a cultural taboo. Gwen resolved to learn all about Indonesia and Indonesian ways.

"I'm going to wait for..." What should she call him? Her dinner companion—creepy. Her boss—too much information. "I'm going to wait."

The waiter bobbed his head and hurried away from the table, never looking at Gwen once.

Gwen glanced at the glittering lights of the archway.

Where was he? Mr. Sunjaya should be back by now.

Minutes ticked by.

Gwen found the Big Dipper in the twinkling lights on the railings. She couldn't imagine what story this might trigger. The whole business of stars as tools to aid memory seemed preposterous. More minutes passed. Gwen stared into her cold coffee, then traced drips of condensation on her water glass. After many more minutes ticked by, she returned her attention to the box.

She tried to read the label. Not one of the words meant anything to her. With false confidence she poked at it, tipping it up on its side and letting it fall.

The man at the next table, the only one still occupied, made the sound of the letter "S" clipped short. "Finish now," he said to his wife, "we're going to be late. Even *you* don't eat this slowly."

"Don't rush me," the woman said. She lowered her voice and said in a whisper, "She's only a girl."

Something inside the box moved around. Whatever it was wasn't packed too well. There didn't seem to be any paper or air packs for shipping. It wasn't heavy, though. It didn't seem to be a rabbit or a kitten or a frog. Whatever it was didn't scurry like it was alive. Gwen pondered the air holes. Maybe it was cheese or something that needed to breathe.

Where was Mr. Sunjaya? It felt like it had been an hour already. Gwen glanced at her phone. Only forty-five minutes. Still, that was a long time.

The waiter cleared the plates from the couple next to her. It was the only table on the patio still occupied. The beautiful woman in the pink cashmere sweater murmured to her husband. Gwen couldn't understand, but when she was a nanny she would learn. Gwen listened, picking out a familiar-sounding word from time to time, but not enough to understand what they were talking about.

The couple rose and walked toward the archway as Mr. Sunjaya had done.

A shiver worked its way through Gwen. The evening was much colder all of a sudden. All the people were gone and the heaters had been turned off. What else could it be?

The woman hung back a little, as if she didn't want to leave yet.

Gwen realized she'd been staring when the woman glanced over her shoulder. She held Gwen's gaze like she was trying to tell her something. It made Gwen so uncomfortable that she had to look away.

When she looked up again, the woman and her husband were passing through the archway. The crunch of their shoes on the gravel grew softer and softer.

Gwen counted the lights as first one then another of the constellations flickered out. Maybe their batteries were dying. She glanced up at the actual sky with the actual stars, but could only see dim faraway flickers. Where was Mr. Sunjaya?

Even though her footsteps were far away, Gwen heard the woman exclaim. A moment later the soft pink of her cardigan and the sheen of her pearls appeared in the archway. The woman rushed across the patio back to her table and grabbed her Prada bag. There was no relief on her face. It was like she'd known exactly where it was all along. As if she'd left it there on purpose. Who would leave a bag like that unattended?

The woman dropped down beside the chair she'd vacated only moments ago and said in a hushed tone, "You must keep it safe and feed it."

Gwen jumped at the sound of her voice. The woman looked out of place squatting between the tables. Someone dressed in such lovely clothes wouldn't hunch down and whisper to a stranger. It made her words carry more weight.

Gwen studied the woman's intense brown eyes. "Me?"

"Yes, you must keep it safe and feed it." She jabbed at the box with a perfect almond-shaped nail. "Or it will turn against you."

An angry crunch, crunch, crunch of leather shoes in the parking lot let Gwen know that the woman's husband wasn't far away.

Gwen reached out for the box and slid it closer to her.

"You feed it, okay." The woman placed her hand on Gwen's leg. "Keep it safe." Her pinky finger was gnarled and mottled and missing from the second joint. She rose slowly. The expression on her face was somewhere between pity and revulsion, an expression that seemed more appropriate from someone who had just seen a horrible accident.

"It belongs to Mr. Sunjaya. He'll be back in a minute."

The woman's eyes reflected the last of the stars still flickering out along the railing. Her eyes glittered as if she might cry.

"He is never returning."

Gwen knew this. She did. She knew it several times over, but she'd pushed the evidence out of her mind. Filled up her head with dreams of her wonderful new job instead.

"How am I supposed to...what is it?" Gwen grabbed the edge of the silver tape and yanked it off.

"No. Feed the jenglot before you look." The woman grabbed Gwen's hand. She held it in both of her own. A faint scent of perfume Gwen had only sampled at cosmetics counters wafted from the woman. She wrapped Gwen's fingers around her water glass and squeezed. The hideous decapitated finger pressed against her.

Gwen tried to pull away, but the woman was stronger than her fuzzy pink sweater would indicate.

"You can be okay. You may survive if you do what I say."

"Wani, come away from her." The man materialized in the archway. "Stop."

The woman didn't flinch at the sound of his voice. She gripped Gwen's hand tighter, squeezed harder.

"Let go," Gwen cried as she scooted her chair back, swung her head around searching for the waiter. The windows were dark and the door closed. Everyone else was gone. "Let go of me."

The woman squeezed tighter.

The man reached out and grabbed her arm.

The glass snapped in Gwen's hand. Water splashed over her arm. Shards of glass tinkled as they hit the floor. A stream of red welled from a gash in her finger and blossomed over her skin.

The woman pulled Gwen until her hand was over the box. Blood dripped onto the cardboard. The woman jerked Gwen so the drips fell through an air hole. "Feed it every day, every day, every day. Never miss a day." She squeezed Gwen's finger tight. Blood drops fell faster and faster.

"The jenglot will help you get whatever you want, but you must never forget."

Tears streamed down Gwen's face. "That hurts."

Nothing moved in the box. Nothing scurried or scattered or erupted in a puff of smoke. Nothing happened at all.

"I know," the woman said. "It will always hurt."

"Let's go now, Wani. There's nothing more you can do." The man put his arm around the woman's shoulders and guided her away. He never once looked at Gwen.

"I could call the police, you know." Gwen applied pressure to her finger to stop the bleeding. "You assaulted me," she called after the woman. She knew she would never do this. Even though the accident was not an accident, in her heart she knew the woman was trying to help her. How and why, Gwen couldn't be sure.

The woman glanced back. "Never forget to feed it."

As their feet crunched across the gravel, Gwen heard a sob and maybe she heard, *a careless girl like her is doomed*. Or maybe she didn't, because how would she know?

All of the constellations twisted around the rail had gone out. A grim darkness that only dwelled in the unlit corners of cities flooded the patio and spilled out into the night.

Gwen checked her watch. The hour had passed when the sheriff had locked up her apartment. She lived in the darkness now. She gripped the tape and ripped it off the box.

Big glassy eyes, almost human, stared up at her from a face made from something like desiccated leather, or like a mummy Gwen had seen in a museum once, with ropey muscles and bone-thin arms and legs, as stringy as forgotten turkey wings from the back of the fridge a month past Thanksgiving. Its black hair, human hair, fell over its eyes in a tangled mop.

Gwen reached into the box and picked up the figurine. It was warm to the touch like a living thing.

66

"If you want to reach for the stars," the jenglot said in a dusty old voice, "I will help you reach them."

Gwen nearly dropped the doll. She hadn't seen its mouth move, but maybe it had. Maybe it had moved just the tiniest bit. Nothing seemed impossible.

"What do you want from me?"

"To be safe and well-fed."

"Me too. That's exactly what I want." Gwen's heart fluttered in excitement. She'd found a kindred spirit. "We're going to be wonderful friends."

"You'll forget about me before long."

"I won't forget. Not ever," Gwen said.

"Oh, yes you will." The jenglot cackled its dry, dusty old-woman laugh. "Yes, indeed you will."

Mountain

F rost forms around the edges of the plate glass window and en-
croaches on the Christmas scenes painted with tempera. The
meaty paprika smell of chili bubbling in a steel pot hangs thick
in the air. A sizzle and a curl of steam rises from a pile of home fries piled
in the corner of the grill. Two regulars sit at their individual tables, close
enough to chat. The winter sun glints off their well-oiled hair as they
sip the thick coffee that isn't on the menu and curse the fact they can't
smoke inside anymore. These sights, sounds, and smells are as snug as an
old winter coat, as familiar as home.

Nyla's been away at school. She hasn't given a thought to the diner
where she'd worked all through high school until a few minutes ago,
when she'd turned into the parking lot.

First semester classes had been harder than she expected. *Intro to Psychology* hadn't been so bad, but the math and the chemistry... She hadn't
had time to hang out with all the new friends she didn't make because

she had to study so much. Her own fault, really. She probably should have taken some "easy A" classes. That's what other people do. She is definitely going to remedy that situation during the spring semester. Nyla's a little taken aback by how melancholy the diner makes her feel, like she's been yearning for the good old days when everything had been easy, and she just hadn't known it.

Nyla steps past the silver Christmas tree with the porcelain angels and blown-glass sailing ships, and slides into the employees' booth in the corner. She shrugs out of her quilted coat and stuffs her gloves in her pocket.

Pushed up against the wall, a soup bowl filled with water holds a wooden cross with fresh basil wrapped around it. It's to sprinkle a house on the days between Christmas and Epiphany. It's supposed to keep the hobgoblins from rising from their underground lairs to find a body to inhabit. Sprinkling is supposed to keep them out of the house. It's a dumb superstition. Only people from the mountains would actually believe children born this time of year would turn into hobgoblins. Eleni and Nick are nice, but they're a little backward. She's never seen the sprinkling cross in a restaurant before. Odd.

From habit, Nyla grabs a knife, fork, and spoon from the gray plastic bin and rolls them in a red cloth napkin. Before she's even rolled her second set, Eleni pushes through the swinging door. When she turns, her face explodes with an expression that looks like alarm, but quickly resolves into an expression of joy.

"Nyla!" Eleni rushes over and throws her arms around Nyla's neck. "You're home!"

Nyla stands to better return her hug as Eleni kisses her on each cheek.

"Look at you. Look at you!" Eleni grins at her like they're best friends.

Nyla and Eleni are friends, but not best friends. They don't have enough in common. Eleni lives like she never came down from the mountain or moved to America. Nyla doesn't have much patience for that.

"Look at you! So skinny," Nyla says. "You had the baby."

Skinny is a bit overstated. Eleni is on the heavy side even when she isn't pregnant, and this had been her second. She's way too young to have two kids already. She's a year younger than Nyla, and Nyla can't even imagine having a husband and children. It's a shame, really. Nick is such an old man. You can take the girl off the mountain, but you can't take the mountain out of the girl.

"You don't have to do that." Eleni took a roll of silverware from Nyla. "You don't even work here anymore."

"Boy or a girl?"

"Boy."

Something in Eleni's voice hitches just the tiniest bit. Something's wrong. Most new mothers would have had the pictures out already.

"Congratulations!" Nyla plops down in the booth and reaches for more silverware.

Eleni looks so much older than nineteen. Mostly it's the frumpy clothes she wears. If she'd try a little harder, she could be cute. Nyla thought how it might be fun to take Eleni shopping. Nick probably wouldn't go for that. Men from the mountain want their wives to be good cooks and their girlfriends to be pretty. Poor Eleni. She could have gone to college and had a good life, but she'd settled for this instead.

"Sophie must be so excited to have a little brother," Nyla says.

"Yep," Eleni's eyes dart to the left then hover in the middle, as though she's fascinated by the ornaments on the Christmas tree. She tucks her hair behind her ears with a twitch of her wrist.

Is she lying? Everything Nyla has learned so far in her Intro to Psychology class seems to point in that direction. Eleni won't make eye contact. Why would she lie about whether Sophie likes the baby? What four-year-old wouldn't be thrilled to have a new baby in the house?

"You look great!"

Eleni slides into the booth across from Nyla and rolls her eyes.

Up close, Eleni doesn't actually look all that good. Her skin is sallow, and the circles under her eyes look like the bruises Nyla got once when she was too close to her brother's game and got whacked in the head with a hockey stick. When she leans down, Eleni's hair falls forward. Patches of bare scalp she'd obviously tried to hide are exposed.

Nick is a jerk sometimes, but he wouldn't hit Eleni. Nyla looks through the window into the kitchen. She catches his eye, and he waves at her. Something's a little off with him, too. He looks bleary-eyed, like he's been living on coffee and cigarettes for a week. Still, he wouldn't give Eleni a black eye. Nyla'd known Petra for years, Nick's first wife. Petra had trained Nyla as a waitress. She was a mean one, always finding fault and complaining. Nyla had been happy when Petra had left Nick for a man with more money. Nick and Petra had fought constantly, but he never once hit her. She'd have known if he had, Petra would have broadcast *that* to the world.

"Did you have a good Christmas?" Nyla asks.

"Oh yes, cooking was hard because I was so..." She makes a gesture to indicate a pregnant belly.

"Wait. What?" Nyla glances down at the wooden cross in the bowl of water. "When did you have the baby?"

"Two days after Christmas." Eleni looks deep into Nyla's eyes, as if the words mean more than they seem and she's trying to see if Nyla understands.

"You had the baby," Nyla counted on her fingers, "three days ago?"

Eleni nods.

"What are you doing here?" Nyla is horrified. Mountain people are so damned backward.

Eleni doesn't reply.

"But you have a newborn."

Eleni snaps her head in a perfunctory nod and pushes her lips into a thin line, as though she's made a decision and isn't going to be persuaded otherwise.

Something tightens in Nyla's stomach. Sometimes women get depressed after giving birth. Someone like Eleni wouldn't know how to treat depression.

"You found a sitter for Sophie and the new baby? Good for you. You probably needed the break." Christmas was the hardest time of year for women who went the traditional route. All the cleaning and cooking. It must be exhausting, although coming to work at the diner didn't really sound like much of a getaway.

"Sophie is with my mother."

"The *children* are with your mother, you mean." Nyla turns the wooden cross over in its bowl of water. Like a cloud had moved in front of the sun, the mood in the diner darkens.

Something is wrong, Nyla's instincts are telling her. She has excellent instincts, her high school counselor had said, which is why she'd decided to major in psychology. If Eleni needed her help, she would definitely get it.

"Who's with the baby?" Nyla asked.

"It was born three days after Christmas and nine days before Epiphany."

"Who's with the baby, Eleni? Where is the baby?"

"It is..." Eleni lowers her head. Her hair falls forward, exposing a patch of bare scalp. "Cursed by Saint Basil." The words escape from her like air from a balloon. One tear, then another, drips onto the shiny table.

Stupid old wives' tales. No one believes them, not here in the States. No one believes them but mountain people. Newborn babies don't have the brain capacity to act crazy. They can't harm their siblings or their parents. They're just babies. It doesn't matter if they're born when hobgoblins are supposedly running free. They're helpless little things.

"You can't leave a newborn alone," Nyla whispers. "You can't do that. Tell me you didn't do that." Stupid backward mountain people. Nyla wants to slap the stupid out of her.

Eleni stares into Nyla's face, her mouth open but unable to say a word.

Little by little, she crumples until her head falls to the table and sobs wrack her body.

"You'll go to prison." Nyla thrusts her arms into her coat sleeves and jumps to her feet. She grabs Eleni's arm and drags her out of the booth. "You can't leave a baby alone."

"What's happening here?" Nick storms through the swinging door, slamming it into the wall. Splotches of sauce and grease stain the apron pulled tight across his belly.

"Eleni and I are going to check on the baby." Nyla tries to make her voice sound strong. The old men at the tables by the window avert their eyes and study the contents of their cups, reading the grounds, staring far into the future.

Nick's eyes flare with anger. Nyla shrinks away from him.

"No. Leave that child be." Nick paces toward the women, arms raised as though he's going to squeeze them in an enormous bear hug.

"I'll call the police." Nyla holds up her phone with her finger poised to dial. A flicker of doubt enters her mind. Maybe her knowledge of psychology isn't enough to help Eleni and Nick. She doesn't get to co-dependence and enabling until next semester.

Nick's arms deflate incrementally until they're in a position of surrender, as if he's envisioning the police stepping through the door.

"You're going to take me to see the baby and that is my final word." Nyla considers stomping her foot for emphasis, but the moment has passed.

Eleni looks up at her husband with a tentative, pleading expression.

Eleni is so weak. Nyla is never going to defer to her husband like that when she gets married.

Nick studies Nyla for an instant. He smiles, just a little, like he's glad to have someone competent in charge for a change. Of course, he would feel that way. Nyla's almost family. If anyone can make this right, she can.

"Go, then." Nick snaps his head forward in assent. He wipes his hands on his apron and turns toward the kitchen.

Eleni threads her arm through Nyla's and grips her harder than is necessary. She pulls Nyla toward the swinging door.

"Where are we going?" Nyla asks.

"The cellar." Eleni kicks open the door like they both had done a hundred times when carrying a full tray.

"The baby is in the cellar?" Nyla can't decide which is worse. Leaving a baby alone to fend for itself, or keeping it in a dank cellar with the root vegetables and rats. "Why, Eleni?"

"I don't know what else to do." Eleni drags Nyla through the steamy kitchen until they stand in front of a scarred wooden door with a padlock.

"You need help, Eleni," Nyla says. "I can find you a counselor, a doctor. Everything will be okay." She's sure of it. Nyla puts a hand on her friend's shoulder. There are so many great treatments for depression or whatever it is that's wrong with Eleni.

Eleni doesn't respond.

"Let's just make sure the baby is okay. Did you burn his feet until the toenails turned black?" Stupid, stupid barbaric rituals like this have no place in the modern world.

Eleni's face trembles like she's going to cry. "It didn't do any good."

"Oh no, Eleni." Nyla imagines herself in court as the expert witness, explaining how her friend is mentally ill and not responsible for falling prey to the superstitions from the barbaric poverty-stricken mountain country. She doesn't know, Nyla would explain, that we have better ways to deal with depression. Nyla feels sure she'll be able to save her friend. Keep her out of prison, at least, if not a mental health facility. There are worse places.

Nyla watches as Eleni fishes out the key that hangs on a string around her neck. She inserts it in the padlock and turns, then lifts the lock from the hasp. Eleni grips the door knob and pushes the door open. Damp cold air tinged with the green smell of sprouted potatoes rushes over them.

There are worse places.

"You go," Eleni says.

Nyla hesitates a moment. She draws in a deep breath and listens. She doesn't hear anything. Not a cry or a murmur. She braces herself against the specter of the newborn dead from the burns to his feet. Stupid, stupid ignorant peasants.

Tears well in Nyla's eyes. She's a professional, almost. She can do this. She has to do this. She pulls the string swaying in the drafty air. Feeble light spills into the basement.

"Nyla," Eleni whispers.

Nyla turns.

Eleni pushes the wooden cross with the basil into her hands. Regret and sorrow twist her features. Of course she's sorry. Eleni isn't an evil person. Nyla makes a mental note to emphasize that when she testifies as an expert in court.

As soon as Nyla takes the cross, Eleni backs into the kitchen. She slams the door.

Nyla jumps. For a minute she wants out of the cellar more than she's ever wanted anything else. She should never have come here at all. She should have just stayed at Plattsburg and worked through the holiday break.

In a moment, though, Nyla has come back to reality. She stuffs the stupid cross in her pocket and braces herself. Ignorant superstitions from ignorant people. Each stair creaks like a crying baby as she steps on it, which only emphasizes the absence of the actual baby's cries. As she reaches the bottom, the smell of sprouted roots and dirt intensifies and mingles with the oily, moldy smell found only in roughly finished rooms baffled from the outside world by a blanket of snow. She steps into the basement, afraid to open her eyes. Afraid to witness the horror that is just a blink away.

The seconds tick by.

Nyla forces her eyes open.

They fall on a shelf with industrial-sized cans of soup, corn, carrots, shortening. She turns. Bins of potatoes, onions. Bags of rice, flour, barley.

The motor in a chest freezer whirs. Nyla jumps so hard she nearly wets herself. Her heart pounds. The earthy damp surrounds her, closes in on her. She struggles to catch her breath.

Where is the baby? Nyla's eyes fall on the smooth expanse of the freezer.

Her heart skips a beat. Her throat tightens. They wouldn't. Eleni would never...

With tiny shuffling steps, Nyla approaches the freezer.

She places her hand on the cold top. Hesitates.

I won't tell them in court where I found the baby—unless they ask. I'll talk about post-partum depression and how successful the new SSRI drug treatments can be and how family counseling... Eleni might not get life in prison. She might not get the death penalty.

Maybe she deserves it. Maybe she deserves it even if she is mentally ill. Nyla slides her hand into place to open the freezer. Who could do something so horrible to a baby?

Just as she works up her nerve to open the freezer, she turns her head ever so slightly and catches sight of a basket on the floor, right in front of the dryer by stacks of laundered aprons. Nyla's breath comes out in one big gush. The heat from the dryer might have kept him warm.

She rushes to the basket. Looks inside.

Nyla's senses narrow. All the damp and smells and whirring and humming fade into the distance.

He's tiny, but perfect.

Nyla falls to her knees.

He clutches his little fists to his chest. His legs lie perfectly posed, like a sleeping baby in a Renaissance painting.

Is he sleeping? Please, please, please be sleeping.

His tiny toenails are gray, black in some places, but he doesn't look seriously burned. No blistering, no swelling, no peeling skin. His little blue eyelids are closed. His lips, lavender pink and bow-shaped, are impossibly small and still. Wisps of black hair cover his baby head and curl around his face.

Nyla reaches out. She moves as slowly as she can. In the moments before she touches him, hope lives. It swells in the basement like a living entity, throbbing like a beating heart.

She touches the baby's toe. He's cool to the touch, but not otherworldly cold as she suspects a dead body would be. Nyla pinches his little thigh gently and wiggles.

The baby doesn't kick or turn or make sucking movements in his sleep like other babies. He doesn't move at all. Nyla leans close to see if she can see his chest rise and fall.

An unfathomable sadness washes over her. The cold, damp earthy smell, the smell of the grave, rushes in.

She slides her hands under the cool flesh that was once the embodiment of joy and potential and scoops the baby up. He flops against her chest. His top-heavy head with the soft black curls rest against her cheek. She holds him against her. Wraps her coat around him and weeps as she rocks him back and forth like he'd never been rocked in his tiny life.

When the baby stirs, Nyla is rocking too intensely to notice right away. By the time she realizes he's squirming in her arms, she doesn't have time to fully process her joy before the baby unclenches its fists and plunges its claws into her belly.

The pain sears like no pain she'd ever felt, burning in her intestines, raging in her chest. She tries to push the thing off, but it clings to her, digging in deeper and nestling in the cavity it carves out.

Nyla opens her mouth to scream. Before the sound comes out, the baby's blue eyelids flutter open. It locks Nyla in its gaze, piercing her with its red hobgoblin eyes. It opens wide and clamps its fangs around her windpipe.

As the room fades to gray, then to black, and the intense pain finally gives way to a merciful numbness, Nyla realized she should have listened to her instincts and just stayed at school.

Fairy Lights

Candlelight is never as great as it is in theory. Its inconvenience outweighs its charm every time. Nutmeg and spice simmering in a pot on the wood stove scent the air, nice and homey, but under the cheery smell something is off, as if one of the ingredients had gone just a tiny bit rotten.

Down the hall, Hadley and Ridley are asleep in their bunk beds. Hadley's first lost tooth is stuffed under her pillow. Ridley, who lost her second a week ago, had plotted with her sister to catch a peek of the tooth fairy. At five, they still believe. Believing is torture. The excitement on nights when magical beings are supposed to appear is as tangible as ants in the bed. They've tried all the tricks to stay awake to see the fairy, but in the end, they've succumbed to the sleep that no child ever thought would come and are quiet at last.

A groan, like an ogre awakening, rumbles up through the floor. The sound grates in Molly's chest like one ragged edge of a broken bone grinding against another. No one else ever seems to hear it. None of the neighbors complain. Adam says it's probably the building settling or the wind or something. Molly hears the sound most often late at night, when she's the only one awake. She really does hear it, even if nobody else does.

The building is old. Do buildings settle forever?

At the end of the hall, where the cathedral window looks down on the cityscape that had added several thousand dollars to the mortgage on their condo, something pings against the glass. A bug, maybe. Probably. They're too far from the street for a car to throw a pebble.

"Adam." Molly places her goblet of Cabernet on the glass-topped table next to her husband's clutter of pocket stuff and bounces on the sofa. He always seems to leave a mess wherever he goes. Nothing major anymore, not like the squat-hole of an apartment he'd lived in when they were dating, just enough to disturb the aesthetics of the room.

Adam's head bumps against the little wooden knob on the sofa's arm. "Uh huhhh... mmm."

Like a nervous tic, the impulse to rub his head and make it better nags at her. She doesn't do it, because that would be dumb. He isn't five. A little knock on the head would be nothing to Space Ghost.

Her husband is still dressed in most of his work clothes: wilted white dress shirt, loosened tie, top button undone on his slacks. He works a lot of hours at a job he says he doesn't like, but he really does. His slacker aesthetic has morphed into something respectable. He talks about his job with the same hyperactive mania that used to take him over when he talked about music. He's the one adult she ever seems to talk to anymore, if talking describes what it is they do.

Adam has succumbed to the magical sleep that he too had believed would never come. He's a high-energy guy. That's what attracted her at first, although his sleep is more pharmaceutical than magical. That part hasn't changed. Adam seems to think he suffers from insomnia, but Molly can't remember a night lately when he's been awake past ten. He deserves to sleep. He works hard, and pays for all the things Molly likes. But honestly, this is getting ridiculous.

"Space Ghost," Molly leans over and whispers in his ear. "Let's watch a movie."

He doesn't move.

A groan rises up all around her. The reverberation enters her through the soles of her feet and shudders through her body. She shakes Adam. "Do you hear that?"

Molly stares at his slack mouth. The string of drool dribbling down his cheek reminds her of the girls when they were babies. She doesn't exist solely to wipe up drool. Does she? Molly pinches him on the thigh hard enough to leave a mark. In spite of the time he spends at the gym, his muscles aren't hard like they once were. He doesn't dance until dawn anymore.

Still nothing.

She picks up the remote and glances at the time in the corner of the oversized TV screen. Eleven p.m. used to be the time when things got started. Whatever happened to that?

Something else hits the window, then again. Ping. Ping.

A new noise. *I'll bet this is the building settling too.*

Molly clicks off the TV.

Listens.

Adam breathes in, out.

At the end of the hall, her sliver of skyline sparkles like fairy lights against the winter sky, reassuring her that life does indeed continue beyond the confines of her condo.

Molly stands up.

Crosses the room.

Enters the hall.

She pauses at Hadley and Ridley's door. Silence. Not a rustle or a snore.

The quiet quivers around her, like a glass teetering moments before it falls. She tenses and takes a step toward the window.

"Owww!" Something bites into her foot. She stoops down and scoops up the thing she'd stepped on. Kids and their crap.

A bead.

A tiny letter block.

The letter P.

Smaller than Molly allows the girls to play with, even though they're probably old enough not to choke on things anymore. A foot away is another, L. Like a trail of bread crumbs, she finds the next, U.

Ping.

Louder this time.

The city lights throb brighter for an instant. Just one or two beats of a heart. A trace of red one way, white the other, snake around skyscrapers, leaving trails of color in their wake.

Molly bends down and picks up the bead, R.

Peace, Love, Unity, Respect.

"Damn it." *Can't I keep one thing for myself?*

Hadley and Ridley had gotten into her box of keepsakes. Molly stomps into her bedroom. She lets the beads fall onto the bedside table, yanks open the closet door, and pushes her clothes out of the way.

In the back corner of her closet, behind the box of clothes that no longer fit, she finds a box tied with a ribbon. She slides to the floor, cradles it in her lap and opens the lid.

A tangle of candy-colored bracelets are just as she's left them. Molly slips one on. She admires the sparkly blue eyelashes, a tube of neon-pink lip gloss, kaleidoscope glasses, bows and trinkets and blinking bunny ears, bandannas, fishnet gloves, her furry hat. A big heap of junk. It looks so silly and childish.

From its spot tucked in the corner of the box, Molly plucks a plastic baggie with a smiling fairy printed on it. She holds it up to the light. The powder is gray and grainy. She opens it and sticks her tongue inside. A candy smell hits her nose as the bitter sting makes her eyes water. "Silky Chan," she whispers.

"Yup."

Molly spins her head around then jumps to her feet. She opens her mouth to say something, but so many words flood her head she can't get any to come out.

Silky looks just like he had the first time she'd seen him: bare-chested, wing tattoos down the length of his arms, pants riding low beneath his prominent hip bones, lank hair falling over his eyes. His face is too pretty for a man, too chiseled for a woman. Molly's heart thrums.

The building groans. The sound aches in her more than it ever had before. It lingers and lingers until it infuses the air with anxiety.

"Molly, girl. Was that Space Ghost I saw laid out on your couch?"

"Adam doesn't go by that name anymore."

"Oh, no? He's not a DJ anymore?" Silky raises an eyebrow, which gives his face a sly, impish quality.

"We're married. He's got a real job."

"That's not the Molly I know. Give me a fucking break."

"You're the one who left, you know." Molly puts her hand out and touches Silky's cheek. It's fleshy and warm, not at all what she expects.

"Space Ghost, damn. He always *was* boring." Silky pulls Molly to him and hugs her. "Want to go dance?" The heat of him wraps around her and takes the edge off the groaning that seems to be inside as much as it is outside Molly's body.

"I can't, Silky. The kids are sleeping."

"Whoa, *you* have kids?"

"They're great kids," Molly says as she conjures an image of her two little girls with their unconscious heads on their pillows. Ghosts of them spring up from their beds, jumping and squealing and pulling each other's hair.

They aren't always little monsters. Not always.

"If they're sleeping, that's an argument for, not against." He flashes his sweetest grin at her. His lips are the frosting rose on the most luscious birthday cake ever, his teeth flawless pearls in a row.

"I'm in my pajamas."

Silky places his hands on her hips and lets his eyes graze over her. "Perfect."

"I—"

"Stop looking for reasons to say no. Don't you love me anymore?" He holds Molly's gaze.

She sinks into the depths of his doe-like anime eyes. The excitement she finds there is contagious. No one will notice if she goes out. Just for a little while.

"Okay. Let's go."

Silky Chan grabs her hand.

Molly snatches a handful of candy bracelets, the baggie with the fairy designs, and her coat before he pulls her into the hall. Molly's socks slide on the polished floor. "Shhh. Don't wake them up."

Silky hoots as he shoves the back door open and throws his leg over the banister. Molly scrambles down the stairs, trying to keep up with his unsteady slide to the bottom.

"Careful," she warns. She tries her hardest not to imagine Silky's broken body lying at the foot of the stairs.

Silky's broken body... *What an idiot*, Molly thinks. When did she turn into some old lady grump who's afraid of every little thing?

"I hate being careful!" Silky dismounts with a mischievous grin and shoves his way through the door into the night. "Whoo!" he yells as he scoops Molly up and spins around with her. He seems impervious to the cold.

The city lights sparkle against the velvet sky in a kaleidoscope of color. The air is tart and sweet like a caramel apple. The hum of the city thrums with music played just for her. Every single thing is a perfect instance of itself, from the glowing street lamp to the cantankerous hot dog vendor giving them the evil eye to the perfectly formed neon of the sign in the window of the corner store. The city is as charming and as precious as an illustrated story book.

How long has it been since she's been outside? She hasn't been shut in more than a day or two. She's gone to the grocery. Taken the girls to the park. How is it possible that the city spinning around her is an entirely more lovely place tonight? Has she really been trapped so completely in the cocoon her life has become?

Silky takes her hand and runs, pulling her along. They weave around the idyllic folks in their woolen coats and long scarves as they sip steaming beverages and lean their heads together, earnestly discussing topical topics.

Are there always people on the street this late?

Silky and Molly dart between parked cars and into traffic. A car honks, just as cars always do in these cases. An irate driver shakes his fist in their direction and yells a mild obscenity. Silky laughs his pleasing melodic laugh and runs faster.

In no time at all, the joy of moving her muscles and running full out causes Molly to stop wondering why a driver would have his window open at night, in November. She forgets to look for other bits of evidence that something isn't quite right with life on the street.

Breathless, they come to a stop at the door of *Liberation*. The thump, thump, thump of the music swells the seams of the building and pulses out through the cracks. A halo from a street light casts a hazy aura around Silky. His cherubic cheeks are flushed. The light falls just right on his tawny skin, making him look like he's made of marzipan. He is a perfect instance of himself.

"Do you love me?" Silky throws his arms around Molly and pulls her close. The candy scent of him entwines around her. The throb of his heart beats with hers. No building is groaning and moaning here. No settling is going on.

Silky Chan is the first one who ever made her heart flutter. The first one who filled up her daydreams. Even though she's married to Adam, loves Adam, her love for Silky will always be inside her somewhere, hidden away, like the trinkets in the box in her closet. Every love is different.

Every love is precious. She never loved anyone with such fearless abandon as she'd loved Silky.

"I do," Molly whispers into his mouth.

"Do you love me forever?" Silky slides the words into her.

The door swings open, pushing them aside before Molly commits herself to forever. The music throbs and prods and drives them inside.

As though carved from the earth, the interior of the club is brown and woody, dank with humanity and desire. The lights pulse. Dancers bounce and roll and spin into a river of flesh. They form a body, break apart, and come together again. All of the dancers are a piece of the unified whole.

Molly lets the river of music carry her. Silky ebbs away and flows back to her. Lights swirl, irresistible beats drop. The *one* of music and people and time swells into an orgy of motion. Hours pass, hours and hours pass into the river music.

Peace, love, unity, respect...

*   *   *

Damp with sweat, Molly finds herself deposited like sludge in the alley behind the club. Her teeth throb in time to the ache in her head. The halos around the city lights have a hard edge to them and something not quite pink, more of a brown, seeps into the sky from the horizon. It can't be that late. Molly feels in her pockets for her phone. She finds her change purse with a few crumpled bills and some quarters, and a lemon drop with a fleck of tobacco on it. She puts it in her mouth as she walks up to a figure slouched against a Dumpster.

"Do you know what time it is?"

The man doesn't acknowledge her. He doesn't move at all.

Something Molly can't be sure of shifts and casts a rippling shadow over the body huddled with his knees rigid against his chest. The flicker of dark and light accentuates his unnatural stillness. All the sounds of the city pause for an instant, a glass teetering before it falls.

Molly's chest tightens. She waits for the shoulders to rise with a breath.

She waits.

Waits.

"Hey." Molly squats beside the man. She turns his head.

Lank hair clings close to his skull. Wing tattoos spread down the length of his veined and scabby arms. He lifts his head. His face—too pretty for a man, too chiseled for a woman—is distorted and hollow, just a shadow of what it had once been, as though he'd stayed so long at the party he'd ground the planes of his face to an uneven pulp.

Eyes as flat and expressionless as sludge stare at her from sunken sockets. Silky opens his mouth. His teeth, no longer pearls, stand ragged and rotten, guarding the chasm of his mouth.

He emits a groan. The sound has found her. It's been Silky all along. It rumbles from him, through the conduit of the building that is her home, and into her. The sound comes to a grinding halt in Molly's chest. She stumbles back, shocked by the desire and desperation of it. "Peace, love, unity, respect," he croaks out the weatherbeaten party mantra.

She should go home now.

Now.

Everything may not be lost.

Molly backs away. First one step, then another. Bits of gravel tear at her feet through her socks.

"I know you've missed me," Silky groans as the specter of him stumbles and rises. "You know how to make this better." The sound of his voice rattles Molly so hard she nearly falls. She's horrified by how much she wants to cuddle up next to him. Silky unfurls his tattered and stinking fairy wings. He reaches out for her. Slips his fingers into her pocket and pulls out the baggie with the fairies. Molly gasps as Silky surrounds her with his fetid desire.

"Stay with me." He kisses first one cheek, then the other. "You'll stay if you love me."

She rips the baggie from his grasp, tears it apart, and watches as the fairies flicker away.

She turns.

She runs.

Silky groans and wails and keens as his facade crumbles. Bit by bit he collapses into a heap of feathers and hip bones and tarnished, impish grins.

Molly buttons her coat against the cold November air and points herself toward home. She digs around deep in her pocket for her one-day chip.

* * *

Adam stares at Molly as she stands in the doorway and asks to come in. With disbelief as tangible as broken glass, and a disappointment so sharp Molly can taste it in the air, he says, "Where have you been?"

"I had to go out."

"Oh, no, Molly. Please, no."

Molly looks down at her filthy pajamas and her ruined socks.

Believing in magical beings is torture.

"I'm back now, Adam." She holds up the chip. "I'm not going again. You have to believe me. I sprinkled his ashes. He's all the way gone."

By the Book

A draft swirls through the room, which was once a parlor but is now a living room. A room for the living. The breeze lifts the filmy curtains which should be, to be true to Victorian motif, heavy and velvet. The white sheers are all that's left of Bridget's authentic Victorian window treatment. They float into the room like Ophelia's veils in the river.

The night is too cold for Halloween. Concerned mothers will force their kids to ruin their costumes by stuffing winter coats under their witch dresses or Superman tights. The few mothers who still let their kids trick-or-treat, that is. The cold air is thin. It's a sign that the time is right. The veil between this world and the next must also be thin.

Bridget's living room, which takes up nearly half the space in the first-floor apartment of the old Victorian she rents, is as tidy as a photo in a Pottery Barn catalog. On this particular Halloween eve, it's even more tidy than usual. She's child-proofed it. Every carpet is taped down to prevent falls. No glass knick-knack or sharp-edged object is within reach of anyone under five foot ten. Plastic bags are hidden from every living thing, and even the electrical outlets are protected against the insertion of the stray knife or fork.

A week ago, Bridget had posted a flyer advertising her services as a mother's helper on the bulletin board in the very same library where she had found *the book*. Fewer parents than she had expected stopped by to interview her. Seems like parents would be more enthusiastic about such a fastidious babysitter, especially one willing to work on a holiday. Perhaps they sensed she was trying too hard. So far, she'd only gotten one customer.

One is all she needs.

"That picture of you is creepy," Roderick says.

He bounces on her Chinoiserie-print settee with his arms wrapped around his knees and his shoes on the cushion. He's a chubby boy with red hair and freckles. It's easy to see the balding, overweight, inconsiderate man he'll become.

Bridget wants to kill him.

She's going to kill him tonight when the clock strikes midnight, but if she does it now the task will be over, and his nasty little shoes won't be ruining her expensive furniture. She probably should wait until midnight, though. Everything by *the book*.

According to the mysterious volume that had appeared on the shelf at the branch library between *Victorian Designs for the Home* by Newton, Charles and *Introduction to Victorian Style* by Crowley, David, midnight on All Hallows Eve is the only night of the year when the veil to the otherworld is thin enough to breach. Why would a book like this appear on her favorite shelf? Britney had obviously put it there. There's no other explanation. Her twin longs to return.

The language in the book had been a bit old-fashioned and dense. Bridget had to look up many of the words, but anything worth doing takes effort. She'd pored over the book for months until it became clear what she had to do.

"That's not me." Bridget glances at the studio portrait of Britney. Their appearance is identical. In every other possible way, they're different. Britney is the friendly one, the trusting one, the sexy one—the dead one.

The ghostly sheer curtain catches a draft and wafts into the room. The veil is thin, Britney. The veil is thin tonight. Bridget and Britney will be together again.

The photo's intricately carved frame is beautiful. The photo looks all wrong. It should be in sepia tones. She remembers her sister that way. She has to. The colors are too vivid otherwise. Remembering Britney's colors will make her come undone, and that can never happen again.

"It looks like you." Roderick's feet slide off the cushion and thump on the floor. He propels himself across the room and comes to an abrupt stop in front of Britney's portrait. "Except something's weird about her eyes."

Roderick's mother had warned Bridget about the child's hyperactivity disorder. She'd also said he was prone to putting non-food items in his mouth. Seems an odd thing for a seven-year-old to do, but at least he won't suffer with his afflictions much longer.

Somehow, Bridget will have to deliver the news of Roderick's demise to his mother. That's a troubling thought. She isn't sure what she'll say. The best solution is to let Britney tell her. Britney is good with people.

"She looks like me because we're twins," Bridget says.

The words sound redundant. She'd never had to explain her status before. Everyone, or at least everyone who matters, knows she's a twin. She's the polite one. The cautious one. The serious one. No wonder Bridget feels off-kilter. Together she and Britney are two halves of a balanced whole. Alone, nothing is as it should be.

"Her eyes look otherworldly because she's dead," Bridget says. "The picture is called a *memento mori*. With the advent of photography, Victorians took up the habit of photographing deceased family members to create keepsakes. The practice has fallen out of favor in—"

"For real dead?" Roderick's eyes display the first spark of curiosity Bridget has seen.

"Yes."

"How come she died?" Roderick touches the bowed glass of the portrait. Bridget thinks about telling him to keep his fingers to himself, but she holds her tongue. She'll give her apartment a thorough cleaning tomorrow.

His question is rude and inappropriate. In spite of its thoughtlessness, Bridget prefers it to the fake sympathy and forced condolences most people offer. The answer to that question ultimately lies in Britney's nature. She was the friendly one, the trusting one, the sexy one. That's an open invitation for disaster. How come, indeed?

A glimmer of white behind the leg of the settee catches Bridget's eye. The tiny globe rolls and rolls until it runs out of momentum and stops. Another... It's definitely a sign.

"You'll be afraid if I tell you. It's not an appropriate story for children."

"You can tell me. I played Grand Theft Auto once." Roderick plops down on the edge of Bridget's Queen Anne chair. He bounces up and down.

"This is real, not a game."

"I know that." He fiddles with a tassel on a pillow, almost stands up again, and then falls back. It's probably a symptom of that condition his mother described, but it looks more like some sort of existential angst. Roderick craves something true, some sliver of truth unfiltered.

Roderick reaches over the leather-bound book Bridget found at the library, *the book*, and past the kitchen knife, a stand-in for an athame, and reaches for the plate on the table without asking. "Do these have nuts? I'm allergic to nuts." He grabs one of the soul cakes, which are actually tiny pies in spite of their name, and without even acknowledging the beauty of the star-shaped latticework of the crust, he shoves it in his mouth.

Bridget lowers herself onto the settee. She tries to assume a casual air as she reaches down, but her movements are jerky and halting. For some reason she doesn't want this child to know what she's doing. She doesn't want to let him know how thin the veil is, or how hopeless his situation.

"Ewww." Roderick cups his hand under his mouth and spits. "Nuts, nuts, nuts!" He hops to his feet and jumps up and down as though he has to urinate. He holds the handful of chewed-up mush at arm's length.

While Roderick's occupied with jumping, Bridget snatches up the pearl and slips it into the pocket of her cardigan.

Sixteen. This one makes sixteen.

Bridget rushes to the powder room and retrieves the waste receptacle and a damp towel.

"Discard that." She holds out the basket and waits for Roderick to comply. She wipes his hand.

"I'm going to die. My air passages are constricting." Roderick gasps and clutches his throat. He staggers against the wall like a victim in a horror movie. The movement is a reasonably good re-enactment of how her sister fell. Britney too clutched her throat and made gurgling and wheezing noises, but in Britney's case the sounds weren't caused by constricted air passages. Britney's air passages were severed. Separated. Cut clean through. The forensic examiner, thinking no family members were close by, had speculated about what might be holding her head on her body.

Roderick won't get to perform the scene to full dramatic effect. For that, he'd need to tangle himself in the velvet curtains Bridget discarded when the cleaners couldn't get the blood from Britney's arterial spray out of the gold velvet.

"No one ever expired from eating nuts."

Bridget tilts her head. She hears it. The rolling sound. She hears it again, even over Roderick's commotion.

Roderick stops stumbling and clutching his throat, as though his theatrics are a sweater he can put on or take off as needed. "Yes they do too," he says. "My mom got the principal to ban them from my school."

The sound persists. It doesn't grow louder or softer. It persists.

"I suppose that makes you especially popular with the other children."

Roderick stops mid-gasp. He narrows his eyes and studies Bridget. "They're just a bunch of bullies anyway."

"If you weren't such a monstrous little yob, maybe the kids would like you better."

The boy's mouth falls open and his eyes grow large. "I'm telling my mom what you said. No one likes a potty mouth."

Bridget doesn't bother to respond. He won't be telling his mother anything. Not on this night, or ever again.

Bridget has never been able to locate the source of the pearls. They come from the general direction of the window with the missing curtain.

Finally, it rolls into view. With the deliberation and unswerving inevitability of a train on a track, it comes to rest against the toe of her shoe. This one has a drip of lurid red.

Seventeen.

How many pearls make a necklace?

Roderick no longer gasps or clutches at his throat. His nut allergy seems to have not been that serious after all. He clutches his fists. His face is a little on the pink side, but he doesn't, in fact, appear to be dying. "Do you have any candy? Kids are supposed to get candy on Halloween."

"I made the soul cakes."

"Those are gross."

"Children aren't just handed candy on Halloween. They must to go out and trick-or-treat for it."

"That's too dangerous. The world isn't safe for kids these days."

"Is that your opinion?"

"My mom says that. She said you were going to do fun stuff for Halloween. I sure would like to know when that's going to start."

"You've never been trick-or-treating?"

Roderick sighs like a world-weary old man. "No. I think it'd be worth the risk, but my mom says no."

"She's probably right. We'll have to respect her wishes."

Roderick's face twitches like his insides are clockwork and someone has wound the key. "How come your sister died?" he asks, once his face has tried on several expressions.

"Someone murdered her."

Roderick's mouth falls open and his eyes grow large and round as is his custom, it seems, when faced with reality. "Where?"

"Right here in this very room. In front of the window." Bridget lets her eyes float along with the curtain. "A man who was visiting her got mad and slashed her throat, then stabbed her over and over until he stuck his knife in her heart."

Roderick's breathing is a little irregular. His face looks a bit sweaty and pale. "Was there blood everywhere?"

"Yes."

"Did you see it all happen?"

"Yes, I did."

The sound is different this time. A pearl bounces before it rolls. Without moving her head, Bridget scans the floor.

"What did you do?" Roderick stops fidgeting. He stares at her, his childish cheeks flushed pink.

"What do you mean, what did I do? I was a witness."

Another pearl bounces, then rolls. Still she can't see it.

"You didn't try to stab him or shoot him or jump on his back or anything?"

Bridget opens her mouth to respond. Why has this idea never occurred to her before?

Pearls fall in slow motion, one after another. They bounce and roll, just like they did on that night.

Bridget jumps up. The light grows hazy and bright. Her head tingles. She should have fought him. She should have done something. Is that it, Britney?

Pearls cascade and roll in every direction.

"Candy!" Roderick dives to the floor. He grabs a handful of pearls and shoves them in his mouth.

"No!" Bridget lunges for him. She grabs him around the waist, heaves him up and shoves her fingers in his mouth. "Spit them out." Her voice is high-pitched and panicky. It's not at all like the soothing tone she'd practiced for her babysitting interviews. She shakes him until he spits out the pearls.

"Bad touch! Bad touch. Stranger danger!" Roderick squeals.

"Quiet." Bridget places him on the floor. "I didn't hurt you."

He scuttles backward like a cornered cat until he hits the wall. "I want my mommmmm. I want to go home."

That's not at all the plan for this Halloween eve. Bridget glances down at her athame, her candles placed just so, and *the book*, the miraculous book that tells her everything she must do to bring Britney back.

Roderick cuts his wail short when the doorbell rings.

"Don't move." Bridget points her finger at Roderick, just like the wicked witch she's become.

The moment she pulls the door open, Roderick lets loose a whoop and charges for freedom. He streams through the door and out into the night, knocking down the small visitor standing on the porch.

"Are you okay?" Bridget holds out her hand to help the child up.

"Trick-or treat," he says through the slit in his plastic mask, and holds open a pillowcase.

Bridget scans the street. Roderick has rounded a corner and is nowhere to be seen. No one else is on the street waiting or watching.

"Come inside. Would you like to try a soul cake?"

The little boy steps over the threshold, and Bridget closes the door behind him.

Any child will do.

No Fear of Dragons

I don't like any of the trains, not one bit. The ones at the Seventh St. Metro station are my least favorite of all. They come and go fast, and you can never trust they are going where the sign says they're going. One time I got on one, and it took me so far I think I was in Mexico when it finally stopped. Maybe I was. It took me most of three days to walk home. Three days doesn't sound like much, but a lot can happen. I know that now. Maybe because three is a magic number. Three days is all it takes to make the world a different place.

The sound of trains is awful too. Trains roar like dragons. Can't trust something that makes noise like that. I like to put my fingers in my ears and say la-la-la-la-la until it passes. That's a thing I do.

I come down to the platform every night anyway, even though I don't like it. Somebody's got to do it.

Tonight is no better or worse than any other. The place is the weird electric light color that I've only ever seen in underground places. It's as bright as daylight, but that's the only resemblance. The light makes the edges of the living people look glowy green. Green isn't a good color on most people. A few look okay, especially if they have nice dark skin, but most people just look red in comparison. It makes me think of flu faces that have been sneezing a lot.

There's a breeze blowing through the tunnel, coming from down the hall and up the escalators, I guess. Or maybe the train is pushing it with its nose as it flies down the track. It's hard to tell. There's no smell to the breeze. I can't tell if it's coming from the ocean or the desert. That's another thing I hate about the subway trains and the station. The air is as scrubbed clean as the electric daylight. It gets me all turned around.

As I'm standing on the platform waiting for the four a.m. train, a girl comes up and stands right next to me. There's plenty room on the platform, so this is kind of weird. I don't move away from her, because she knows what she's doing. A person doesn't stand next to someone on an empty subway platform unless they have a reason.

"Hi," I say. "I'm La-la."

She's got red hair in braids. She's too tall and curvy for a hairstyle like that, but it's still cute on her. Her nails are painted with yellow half-moons on a sky of blue polish. I wish we were friends and I could ask her to do my nails like that.

"Hi," she says.

Her voice is raspy, like she needs a drink of water bad. She scrapes her bottom teeth against the yellow moon on her thumb as she looks down the dark tunnel. "You waiting for the train too?"

I nod. "Where are you going?"

"It's time for me to go, you know?" She smiles at me, but it's kind of sad. She looks nice in the station light. It hits her just the way sunshine would.

"Are you going to away to school?" I always wished I could go away to school. That seems so exciting in movies. I was never smart enough, though, to get in somewhere with an entrance exam.

The girl pretends she doesn't hear the question.

"Aren't you going to miss your parents?" I ask.

The girl shrugs. "I guess. I'm kind of too old for that, you know?"

I do know. When I was little I missed my parents a lot, so much that I felt like a sponge someone had stepped on and squeezed all the water out of. But now I don't feel it so bad anymore. I'm still sad that they're gone, but the sadness doesn't pour out of me as fast as it used to.

"I am going to miss my cat, you know." She adds this as an afterthought, flicking her braid over her shoulder. She stops looking down the tracks and looks right into my eyes.

"What's your cat's name?"

"Bodkin. He's got extra toes on his front paws and he really loves peanuts in the shell." She laughs at this, like she can see her little cat with a peanut.

Then I hear it. The dragon is coming. I stick my fingers in my ears and say, "la-la-la-la-la." It helps a little, but not much. The girl pats my shoulder and yells, "It won't hurt you."

I know that's true, but it doesn't always feel that way.

"Bye," the girl says with a wave as the door whooshes open.

She doesn't have a suitcase, I realize. My first thought is to run after her and grab her back. She can't go to school with nothing. She needs pencils, paper, underwear.

When I see her in the window next to all the other faces with the golden light around their heads, I get it. I don't know how I could be fooled like that. I guess it's because I've never seen somebody who had the yellow light on this side of the window before. Seems like I would have noticed she didn't have the green glow of the living when she was standing right next to me. I can't be expected to see everything. I'm not that smart. I wave at all of them, trying to look at every face as the train pulls away. I wave extra hard at the girl with the braids and the yellow moons on her fingernails. She waves back. I wish we could have been friends.

I hate coming down to the four a.m. train, but somebody's got to do it. Someone has to say goodbye before they are gone for good.

"Poor Bodkin," I say out loud, which I try never to do, because people will sometimes be extra mean to girls who aren't very smart, especially if they talk to themselves. "Poor Bodkin. Who's going to give you peanuts?" I feel like a sponge getting squeezed tighter and tighter. It's sad that the girl had to die. But if someone doesn't find Bodkin, it's not going to end well for him either. That just isn't right, because he has no say in the matter.

And then I see the yellow trail. It's just like the light around the sad faces on the train, but it's on the ground and not attached to anyone.

I suppose I've never seen a ghost trail before because I've never met the ghost on the platform before. I follow the trail across the platform, down the hall, up the escalator and out onto the street. If I keep following it all the way as far as it goes, I'm guaranteed to locate that cat.

Like Night and Day

By the late spring, the heat reaches full blaze in Midway, the most southern town in Pickens County. Every living green thing shrivels up and dies, except for a few mimosa trees rattling their seed-pods in the hot wind or a dusty creosote bush here and there.

Patch, Hank Jr.'s dilapidated old coon hound, lies in a spot of shade and keeps one eye trained on the neighbor's yard. He doesn't move much since he run off and got brought back by the new neighbor, Mr. Gaap. All night and all day, all that dog ever does anymore is lay around. That and keep a keen eye on the neighbor. Strange beast, that one.

The sun beats down on Marla Ann's head as she leans on the chain-link fence. Hotter than hell, most folks have said at one time or another. Marla Ann doesn't blaspheme, but she understands the sentiment. By about August, when the heat hasn't let up in almost half a year, nobody has anything that looks like a lawn anymore. Most folks give up on it altogether and decorate their front yards with gravel and wagon wheels and longhorn skulls and such.

When Mr. Gaap moved into Miz Granger's old place, first thing he'd done had been to dig a big hole in the back yard. Seems like he'd have fixed up the sagging roof, or the tore-up driveway buckled from mesquite creeping too close to the house. Guess he has his reasons. Leaky roof doesn't seem so important until the rain falls. Some folks do whatever it is they want and don't feel no shame.

Hank Jr. says Mr. Gaap is going to make himself a swimming pool. He even hired the boy and his best friend Paul Ray to do his digging. Paul Ray smells about as much like a goat as anything could without actually being a goat. Working outside from sunup to sundown doesn't do much to improve the smell.

That lazy kid of Marla Ann's is over at the neighbor's house from morning until night, too. If he learned to apply himself to going to church like he did to digging that swimming pool, he'd be halfway to heaven already. If she didn't know better, she might think that newcomer had put some kind of spell on those boys. But there's no such thing as spells, especially not ones that would make kids work all day and all night like that. Mr. Gaap has some kind of power over them, though. Maybe he's giving them money Marla Ann doesn't know about.

Since they finished cementing the hole for the pool, Mr. Gaap's been running hoses into it non-stop. All day and all night, water running. And he isn't too careful about it, neither. Spray from the hoses splatters all over the place. Mr. Gaap's lawn is as lush and green as velvet, which is a mighty peculiar thing. How can a lawn spring up like that? His water bill must be sky-high. Most folks in Midway are as broke as the Ten Commandments. Must be nice to have enough to throw money away. Must be real nice.

"Hey, Mr. Gaap. Your lawn's looking pretty." Behind him the spray from the hoses spouts up and out over the entire yard, like a pair of watery angel wings. He sure doesn't have the *face* of an angel, not by a long shot. It is bony and angular with a high knobby forehead and a big nose that hooks at the end. He sure isn't much to look at.

Mr. Gaap turns his head in a slow, methodical way. The movement would have been natural if a rattlesnake had done it. Mighty odd way of moving for a man, though. The sun must have caught in one of those water drops because it looks just like his eyes glowed red for a second. "Good afternoon, Marla Ann."

Now, a gentleman would have said *Miz* Marla Ann because that'd be the polite thing to say, even if around these parts her name came out sounding like "Marlan." Mr. Gaap wasn't brought up in Midway and he must have never learned manners. Maybe they don't teach things like that wherever it is he comes from. Seems mighty strange though because according to him he used to be a professor of philosophy or something or other, which is like Bible studies without the Bible, and you think somebody smart enough to teach would be smart enough to know you ought to address a lady in a polite way.

"Hot enough for you, Mr. Gaap?"

"It is rather warm, isn't it?" Gaap says in that funny stiff voice like he has an extra-long stick up his butt.

A native of these parts would know that the answer to that question is a fine opportunity to lighten the mood and share a chuckle. A good answer would be something like, *Yes ma'am, it's hotter'n two goats in a pepper patch*, or some such thing. But if he'd rather forgo being witty, then so be it.

"I've got a little air conditioner that fits in my kitchen window," Marla Ann says. "It's real nice in the afternoon to sit by it and sip on something cool." She holds her eyes open extra wide and looks up through her lashes because Hank Sr., her ex, said one time that her eyes looked pretty when she did that. Mr. Gaap is nothing to look at, but a single girl can't be picky, not in Midway. Hank Sr. hadn't been much of a prize either, come to think of it. "I was wondering, Mr. Gaap, would you like to come sit in my kitchen and have some sweet tea?"

No shame in asking a neighbor to come in from the heat and sit awhile. That's a respectable way to get to know a fellow. None of the old vultures from church would have any cause to gossip about her at the next potluck—not that having a reason is something they even need. They seem to think being divorced is about equal to having leprosy.

"Why, thank you. I think I will join you."

Before Mr. Gaap even gets all his words out, Hank Jr. comes running out of Mr. Gaap's garage. He's holding a shovel like he's a soldier with a bayonet.

"Mom! Don't make an invitation like that!"

Paul Ray trails behind him wearing that T-shirt with the devil star, like he always wears, with loops of hose wrapped around his shoulders. He's sweating 'cause he's a hefty boy who also doesn't know better than to wear black in the summer.

Hank Jr., who's growing up to look a little too much like his daddy, has a truly fearful look on his face. Teenagers, who can understand what is going on in their heads? Soon as they get to that age they are like aliens from another planet. Not that there is any such thing as aliens.

Hank Jr. better not try to screw this up because he's afraid of getting a new daddy or some such nonsense. Of all the things lacking in Midway, eligible bachelors are number one on the list. Mr. Gaap may not be much to look at, but he's got means and a knack for getting things done.

"Shut up, boy. That's no way to talk to your elders."

Mr. Gaap chortles. The sound rises up from him like sulfur bubbles from the bed of the Wakahatchee River. At least he isn't offended by teen-age foolishness.

"He's going to mesmerize my mom," Hank Jr. says to Paul Ray. "We've got to do something."

Mesmerized! Where'd the boy ever get a stupid idea like that? Everybody knows that mesmerizing doesn't work.

Mr. Gaap lets himself through the fence and extends his arm for Marla Ann to take. He is a gentleman, after all. The old-fashioned kind.

Something strange gets into old Patch at just that moment, and for the first time in weeks he jumps to his feet and barks like the end of the world is nigh.

"Ma, no!" Hank Jr. wields his shovel like a club.

Paul Ray throws off the hose looped around his neck like St. Patrick casting the snakes out of Ireland. Not that there's such a thing as a saint, but it's impossible to get through life without hearing stories about them.

Hank Jr. clutches the charm he's taken to wearing around his neck these past few weeks and hollers, "In the name of King Solomon, I command thee to hold thy ground."

Isn't that just like a teenager? How many times had that boy been dragged into church and made to listen? And the only words that ever spilled from his lips are from the Jew section.

Marla Ann feels the blush rise up from her neck to her forehead.

"I apologize for that, Mr. Gaap. Seems Hank Jr. hasn't heard the good news."

"Ho, ho, ho," Mr. Gaap chuckles as he grabs on tighter to Marla Ann's arm.

"Get away from my mother!" Hank Jr. yells as he charges the gate.

Mr. Gaap kicks it shut without turning around.

The fence catches Hank Jr. right in the gut and winds him. Paul Ray runs right into the back end of him. Serves the boys right for meddling where they don't belong.

Patch charges at the fence and throws himself into it. He bounces back and charges again, all the while howling and barking like a hound from hell.

"The guardian of the waters must not leave his post." Mr. Gaap's voice wavers and grows loud, like the sound of a car engine revving up.

Paul Ray's eyes bulge, or maybe the Coke-bottle lenses in his black-frame glasses magnify them.

The look on Hank Jr.'s face is something to see. He looks about as scared as a cat in a dog pound. About time somebody raised his voice to that boy and made him mind. His own father is good for nothing in that department.

Hank Jr. trudges on over back to the pool and sits himself down on the edge.

Mr. Gaap holds tight to Marla Ann's arm. He even opens the back door and holds it for her to go in, like a proper gentleman.

* * *

When Marla Ann answers the knock on the door, she's not one bit surprised to see Brother Del in his white shirt that is more yellow than white at the collar and pits. The vultures from church must have told him Mr. Gaap came inside her house for a visit unsupervised. They've got their noses in everybody's business. No doubt they were peeking out their windows and spying.

All Marla Ann and Mr. Gaap did was to have some tea and cake. Is that a sin? She's an adult, and she should be able to have company without anybody butting in.

Mr. Gaap had talked, the way men do, about his work as a professor. His philosophy job had been all about talking and writing and thinking, rather than building or fixing or making things, which is peculiar for someone living in Midway. But Mr. Gaap is rich enough to fill a swimming pool, so maybe he is doing things the right way.

For a little while, when Marla Ann had been sitting at the table face to face with him, she could see how all his ideas fit together like a puzzle, and for once she felt really smart for being able to follow along.

All of Marla Ann's muscles clench, and a headache bites at the base of her neck. Brother Del is going to have questions. Lots of them. And the funny thing is, no matter how hard she thinks about it, she can't remember the what-ifs and the wherefores of the conversation she had with Mr. Gaap, even though it had all fit together like a puzzle yesterday.

Marla Ann pushes the door wide open. "Come right on in, Brother Del."

No use delaying the inevitable. Whatever Brother Del has on his mind isn't going to go unsaid.

"Is he here now?" Brother Del's face is as serious as Marla Ann has ever seen it. Even more serious than when he preached the Good Friday sermon.

"Who?"

He can't possibly think Marla Ann let a man she isn't married to stay the night. He should have more faith in her than that.

Brother Del scowls and his jowls jiggle. "Your boy." The cloud of righteous indignation rises up from him like a smoke from a campfire. "Him and that heathen Paul Ray have been up to no good, from what I hear."

Of course, Brother Del came over because of the boy. That makes much more sense. That boy needs some direction. He's going to be lucky if Marla Ann doesn't give it to him with a switch.

"So, where is he then?" Brother Del says, setting his jowls to jiggling again.

"This way." Marla Ann leads Brother Del through the kitchen. The cake from yesterday still sits on the counter, wrapped up in plastic. She cracks open the back door that leads out to the carport and pushes it open without making a sound.

Brother Del puts his head so close to hers she can smell the tang of his aftershave.

Marla Ann puts her finger to her lips and pokes her head through the door.

Brother Del pushes up against her so he can see too. The horns on his longhorn belt buckle pressing up against her hip feel way too close for comfort.

"It was you who lost the fucking necklace. You've got to do this part." Paul Ray's big magnified eyes look wet, like he's about to cry. He sits cross-legged on the black futon cushion Hank Jr. rescued from the attic, where Hank Sr. had stashed all the stuff he didn't take with him when he moved out. They'd drug it out to the edge of the carport.

Hank Jr.'s eyes are so big, even without magnifying lenses, they look like they're fixing to pop out of his head. He paces back and forth. "This isn't working out at all like I thought." He stops his pacing so fast that

107

his sneakers squeak on the blacktop. "He keeps on saying I'm the guardian of the water. I didn't sign on for none of that. All I wanted was my dog back."

Behind them the spray of water from the hoses in Mr. Gaap's yard rises up in the air and splashes into the pool.

"You got your dog back. That part worked fine." Paul Ray holds out a tattered bunch of paper with yarn tied through a hole in the corner.

"Now he's even mesmerized my mom." The papers rattle as Hank Jr. tries to hold onto them with shaky hands. "We've got to do something."

Mesmerized! Where'd the boy ever get a foolish idea like that? Everybody knows that mesmerizing doesn't work.

"Go on out," Brother Del whispers. He gives Marla Ann a little shove.

She holds her ground. Seems like a servant of the Lord shouldn't be putting his hands on a lady like that.

"Everything was going fine until you lost the sigil," Paul Ray says. "How could you even do some stupid-ass shit like that?"

"It was stolen."

Paul Ray's pink cheeks turn pinker. "Why didn't you tell me that? Who stole it?"

Hank Jr. twitches his head around and stares in the direction of Mr. Gaap's pool.

"Fuck, man." Paul Ray scrambles to his feet. "What even happens if one of them gets a hold of their own sigil?"

"Your book doesn't say anything about that, huh?" Hank Jr. glares at his friend and balls up his fist. "Maybe you should have bought the real book instead of making that crappy print-out."

Hank Jr.'s face looks like his daddy's used to when he came home after a three-day bender, only even more guilty. That boy knows he's doing wrong.

Paul Ray snatches the papers tied up with yarn out of Hank Jr.'s hand and riffles through them like a badger on a garter snake.

Marla Ann pushes the back door open a little wider and casts her eyes over the whole of her back yard, then lets them wander over to Mr. Gaap's. Be nice to have a gentleman around to take control of this unruly teenager, she thinks.

The smell of the oil that had worked its way into the concrete of the carport is nearly covered up by the sweet vomitous stink of smoke rising from the bubbling block of something Hank Jr. is burning in a little black dish. Probably drugs in there.

Marla Ann has been on the lookout because that boy is Hank Sr.'s son, and now her worst suspicions are confirmed. Hank Jr. is going to turn out like his daddy, probably worse. Anybody can see that's in the cards. Not that cards can tell the future, but anyone could have seen it coming, cards or no.

"I don't want to mess with this anymore," Hank Jr. says.

"What are you, retarded? You conjured him, and now you're going to just let him run free?" Paul Ray tugs the hem of his black T-shirt with the silver pentagram, to pull it out of the crease between his belly and his boobs.

"I don't know what to do." Hank Jr.'s eyes are wild like he has a fever. Probably from the drugs.

"Hurry up and say the spell."

"That's it right there. I got all the proof I need." Brother Del tenses like a coiled spring right behind Marla Ann. "They summoned a devil. I knew it!"

Marla Ann's heart feels like it is fixing to seize up.

Brother Del shoves the door open and pushes her out of the way. She stumbles out into the back yard and nearly falls. That's no way for a man of the church to act.

"Mom, get in the circle," Hank Jr. yells as he motions for Marla Ann to come over. "Before it's too late."

Marla Ann looks around, but can't see one single thing that could be the circle he's referring to. Foolish teenager and foolish nonsense. Probably the drugs are making him see circles.

The spray of water that's been running non-stop all day and all night cuts off. The sound, or rather the lack of sound, is shocking, like diving into deep water.

Real slow, like he's one of them automatons at Disney World, Mr. Gaap rises up from the pool. Like the savior himself, he walks on the water all the way to the edge of the pool. As calm as can be, he steps onto his velvet green lawn.

Mr. Gaap will know what to do about this. He is a gentleman of the first order and he knows about talking and writing and books.

Old Patch growls and snarls and charges at the fence like he wants to tear Mr. Gaap limb from limb.

With a flick of his hand, Mr. Gaap silences him.

Old Patch falls to the ground, still as the grave.

The silence rushes back in. Not a cricket, nor car engine, not one single thing makes a sound.

Marla Ann's heart thumps. Even that is only a feeling and not a sound. Then, far off in the distance, thunder rumbles like rain is on its way.

Brother Del focuses all his attention on the boys. He wears his fury like a mask because he knows right from wrong. It's the most remarkable thing about him. His face says he's been waiting a good long time for his chance to show it. He pulls his portable Bible out of his back pocket and holds it aloft like he is going to smack some sense into the boys with it.

Hank Jr. and Paul Ray stare at Mr. Gaap like they are the ones who are mesmerized.

Paul Ray, as if he got hit in the head with a baseball bat and it woke him up, yells, "Say the motherfucking words and send him back to hell." He shoves the papers into Hank Jr.'s hands.

Mr. Gaap, cool as a cucumber, strolls toward the boys. He has a smile on his lips that says he knows how to handle teenage foolishness.

"Hold up with your devil conjuring," Brother Del hollers. "Hold up or, by God, I will smite you." He waves his little Bible.

Hank Jr. holds the papers like he is giving a speech at the Fourth of

July picnic. "The thirty-third prince has dominion over the southern region of Hell and Earth. He is best conjured when the sun is in a southern Zo-de Ack-el sign. Gaap controls the element of water. He teaches philosophy and can cause humans to love him."

Mr. Gaap chuckles and shakes his head. "Dear boys, you have the words but not the power. *The Lesser Key of Solomon* must be consecrated."

Hank Jr. turns so pale he is almost see-through. "I told you!" he screams at Paul Ray.

"He's lying, stupid! That's what they do." Paul Ray squeals like a little piglet getting ripped from the tit. He snatches the top page from the homemade book and throws it on the ground. "Keep reading."

"Stop!" Brother Del yells like he is getting to the good part of a sermon. "Repent your evil ways."

Hank Jr. pays him no mind and mutters as he reads down the page. "He can deliver familiars out of the hands of other magicians..."

"No!" Paul Ray says.

"Necromancers can summon him with sacrifice and a burnt offering..."

"No!!!"

"Demon, be gone!" Brother Del hollers as he circles the boys like an Indian doing a war dance.

Clouds roil in the sky like they never did before in Midway. This time of year is dry as dust. Strange how clouds can move like that, like they're from a foreign land where clouds move as fast as birds and the air is heavy and thick with moisture.

"His seal is thus and to be made as aforesaid..." Hank Jr. says.

"That's it!" Paul Ray looks like someone drowning who finally caught a breath. "Say that part!"

Brother Del raises his arms. "Be gone, demon!" He turns a shade of red that isn't found in nature, righteous red, as he surges toward the boys with his Bible held out like a club.

"Don't break the circle!" Paul Ray screams as Brother Del catches him around the neck. The Bible falls to the ground and gets shuffled about as they struggle.

On the blacktop of the carport, the boys have drawn a circle and a star and sure enough, they are both standing inside it. Hank Jr. better not think he is getting away with that. He's going to be down on his hands and knees scrubbing that mess off first chance he gets.

Paul Ray squirms, but Brother Del is still able to catch Hank Jr. by the back of his shirt. Paul Ray uses this to his advantage and wiggles until he breaks free. He takes off running faster than any fat kid ever ran before. He jumps over old Patch, still lying motionless on the ground, and flies through the gate. He disappears around the corner of the house.

"Come back here, boy," Brother Del yells after him. "We going to flush that devil out of you!"

But Paul Ray is long gone.

"Your mama will hear about this!" Brother Del yells to no avail.

Brother Del tightens his hold on Hank Jr. "Tell your boy to mind me, Marla Ann!"

"That boy never does listen to me," Marla Ann says, not taking her eyes off Mr. Gaap. A gentleman like that, he could surely set these boys straight.

Brother Del turns himself and Hank Jr. around until he is facing Mr. Gaap. He drags the boy across the velvet green lawn up to the edge of the pool. "Sorry to make your acquaintance under such circumstance," Brother Del says to Mr. Gaap as he clamps Hank Jr.'s head in a headlock, and he thrusts out his hand.

Mr. Gaap shakes Brother Del's hand. "The pleasure is all mine."

Brother Del is a big man, and he's sweating to beat the band. In spite of the clouds and the thunder, it is still a mighty hot day. He eyes Mr. Gaap's pool like a dog with his nose pressed up on the butcher shop glass. "As you probably heard, this boy is in need of a full immersion to wash the evil out of him."

Truth to tell, seems like Brother Del is looking for any reason he can find to jump in that pool, and church work just presented itself. But one person can never know for sure what's in the heart of another.

A smile like the sun coming up in the morning spreads across Mr. Gaap's face. "Be my guest."

"You don't know what you're doing!" Hank Jr. squeals.

"I'm going to consecrate the hell out of you, boy," Brother Del proclaims as he puffs and struggles to get Hank Jr. to the edge of the pool.

"You got to let me recite from *The Lesser Key of Solomon*!" Hank Jr. yells, as if those kinds of words will have influence on Brother Del.

They must not, because the minute they're out of his mouth, Brother Del heaves him into the pool. The pages of *The Lesser Key of Solomon* fly up in the air and float down like leaves. Hank Jr. sinks like a stone, then pops right up again, sputtering and spitting.

Brother Del does a big old belly flop into the pool. The water roils and bubbles like it's a pot on the stove. He grabs Hank Jr. by the hair and holds him under. "In the name of the Father, I command you to exit this boy."

Marla Ann worries that Brother Del is being a little rough, but the boy needs a good baptizing, so she decides not to interfere. Brother Del does a bunch more hollering and yelling at God to come and deliver the demon out of Hank Jr.

Minutes tick by. It seems like the sky goes from light to dark and back to light again, and still Brother Del holds Hank Jr. under.

Thunder rumbles, like the storm is coming closer.

"Let him up, Brother Del," Marla Ann says without much conviction, because she's thinking maybe Hank Jr. needs some extra time under the water. That boy has a lot of his shiftless no-good daddy in him, and in spite of what they teach in the church about how everyone can be redeemed, most people know that isn't really true. The end is always visible in the beginning. Chances are Hank Jr. is never going to make it too far in life. Marla Ann takes comfort in the knowledge that God works in mysterious ways and in the end everything turns out for the best. Maybe Brother Del knows just exactly how long he needs to hold Hank Jr. under water.

Finally, the boy stops flailing and falls limp. The water roils and bubbles and swirls in a circle faster and faster.

Hank Jr. is caught up in it and pulled down into the middle, like a turd in a toilet. Then the water starts roiling and swirling even faster. The sky does the same. The current or something must be really strong, or maybe a twister touched down, because Brother Del spins around like a top. He hollers and screams like nobody's business. In spite of all the noise he is making, he is sucked into the hole in the middle of the pool too.

Soon as he disappears under the water, the storm clouds let loose. Marla Ann creeps up to the edge of the pool and looks in. Raindrops plunk one after another onto the placid surface.

She studies the water. All around her, leaves tremble with the rain. As hard as she tries, she can't seem to recall what is so important about looking in the pool. She's sure just a minute ago everything fit together like a puzzle. But for the life of her, she can't recall how.

Brother Gaap stoops down and scoops up a little black book. He tosses the bedraggled thing into the trash.

"Good day, Marla Ann." Brother Gaap opens his umbrella and holds it over her head.

Rain splatters on the blacktop. White chalk lines that somebody must have drawn run in rivulets down to the street.

Marla Ann turns and looks into Brother Gaap's smiling face. "It's coming a real gully-washer."

"Good for the garden. Good for the crops." Brother Gaap takes Marla Ann's elbow. A rogue ray of sunlight must have caught on a drop of water, because for a moment it looks like Brother Gaap's eyes flash red.

"Good for the crops, it is," Marla Ann says. "You want to come inside for some sweet tea and cake?"

"Why, thank you. That would be very nice."

Brother Gaap is the most gentlemanly man in all of Midway. Nobody in the whole town, from the velvet green hills in the south to the lush woods around the lake, would make a better pastor than Brother Gaap.

A Flicker of Light on Devil's Night

I suppose I should care more, but little by little all the ordinary cares I had before got chipped away.

The girl's teddy bear is wedged in the corner of the floral sofa that was the least ugly one at the thrift store. She's rearranged the cotton cover that's supposed to hide the hideous thing. A beam of October light that seems transported from a Crate and Barrel catalog makes the earth tones I've been trying to decorate with look like they've been rolled around in actual earth. I guess you have to be rich to successfully dye fabric with tea. The bear is wearing the only good pair of earrings I ever owned—will probably ever own, if I'm honest about it. They are gaudy and haven't been in style for years. For a minute I think I can hear the Pink song that was playing the night my ex gave them to me. That night, his eyes glittered as hard as the little stones with his excitement about all his big plans, all the crazy wild things we were going to do.

Nostalgia is stupid. It makes me physically sick. I never listen to old music anymore. I should probably sell the earrings. I forgot I even had them. I've got more important things to care about.

The living room windows vibrate like a bomb just created a concussion. Construction paper bats I cut out with the girl as the boy watched, so the house would look festive, twirl on their fishing line. Their wings cast long shadows across the braided rag rug. I can almost hear wings flapping, announcing the arrival of the dark angel of the cold times. I imagine the whole neighborhood dropping to the pockmarked ground with hands over their bleeding ears. I guess I'm not in a festive mood. There's no reason to look out the window. There's not a chance the angel dropped a bomb. Nothing as definitive as that. It's only kids fighting. Why can't they be happy for ten consecutive minutes?

I stomp through the living room and yank open the door to the attic. "What are you doing?" I try to modulate my voice so the situation—if it *is* a situation, and it probably is—doesn't escalate.

The girl's siren howl barrels down the stairs. It's not the worst kind of scream, the kind that evokes a pool of blood or a bone poking through skin, but it's alarming enough.

"Shut up, you fat-ass cockhole," the boy yells. The attic is his room now because he's too old to share with a kid, and he doesn't care about the spiders. That's the least of what he doesn't care about. "Get out of my room."

"I don't have to. Mommm!" the girl wails.

I march up the stairs. They are hardwood and still shiny at the edges where no one walks on them. They'd be nice if I sanded and refinished them. "What is the problem?" I demand as I squint into the gloom. The floor is rougher up here. It would take a lot to make it nice, a lot more than I could justify spending on a rental. Like fixing a floor is even one of my options. The October sun barely squeezes in through the dormer window. Outside, across the street, a fire burns in a green plastic trash can. The Devil's Night ceremonies are starting before the sun even goes down. I listen for sirens but hear nothing. One little fire is hardly the worst of it. The trash can is one the city owns, heavy and durable. It won't melt right away. Maybe someone will put it out soon. Maybe someone will catch it in time.

"He's going to cut my arm off," the girl says, her voice hitching with her sobs. "He's got a knife."

"How's she supposed to be Furiosa for Halloween if she's got two arms?" The boy flings his dreadlocks, dyed white even though his hair is naturally blond, out of his face and grins at me with that cocky smile he uses when he's sure he's winning an argument. "It'll grow back anyway." He lounges back on the filthy black-and-white checked futon he dragged in from the eviction trash heap next door, in spite of my warning about bedbugs, and slides the tip of a folding knife under his fingernail.

"I don't want my arm cut off," the girl cries. "Even if it's going to grow back." She hugs herself but doesn't run away.

"Arms don't grow back," I say. "You can be whatever you want for Halloween."

Her crying escalates.

I reach for the knife. "Give me that."

The boy snatches it away. His hair swings back, revealing an angry "X" carved over where most people think their heart is. The lines of the symbol are crusted black, as though he's rubbed dirt in the wound. The ridges are raised and puffy-looking.

I am concerned, but it isn't serious enough for an emergency room visit. Antiseptic will fix this, and he's got an appointment with a counselor. It's not all that bad. It can't be. The appointment is in January, so the doctor must think it's okay to wait three months. He wouldn't make him wait if the boy was really sick, if this self-harm was a symptom of something bad.

"What happened to you?"

"The angel Ariel came down and cut out my heart. She said I'd be better prepared to do my work without it." He lifts his chin and stares at me, as if daring me to contradict him. His voice is as deep as his father's. When did that happen?

"He's cutting himself other places too, Mom. I saw him do it."

"Shut up, buttwipe, or I'll cut you too." He sounds like a boy again. The curtain lifted to expose a glimpse of the future has fallen.

"He poops in a jar, Mom." The girl smirks until a pillow whacks her on the head.

I breathe in and in and in. There is not enough air left in the world.

Should I tell him he's confused the name of Gabriel the angel with the name of Ariel the little mermaid? Is this the kind of thing other teenagers say? I'm afraid to ask other parents. I'm afraid to ask. I'm afraid—

"Little snitching bitches get stitches." The boy pounces on her and knocks her onto the disgusting futon.

The girl giggles instead of crying for once. They really do like each other, in spite of the evidence.

"That's enough. Stop using language like that." This is hardly the worst of it, but there are so many things I need to say and to put a stop to, I don't know where to start.

The attic smells of dirty socks and something fermented. I let my eyes crawl across the magpie tangle of clothes, game cards, buttons, dice, shoes, bags, cups, comics, bits of string, feathers, candles, cigarette butts he says were here all along, and shiny unidentifiable detritus. They fall on a two-quart mayonnaise jar. I can't deal with this right now. I can't deal with this. I can't deal—

I don't even know what to say to a kid who poops in a jar.

"Come downstairs. It's time for dinner."

"I want hamburgers," the girl says. She sprints to the stairs. "Hamburgers and french fries."

The boy rolls over on the mattress and closes his eyes.

Somewhere in the gloom of the rafters, the dark angel Ariel flaps her wings to warn of the coming cold times, or perhaps it's a bat. Most likely it's a bat.

"You too. Put on a shirt but don't button it. I want to put medicine on that cut."

"I'm not hungry." He opens one eye and looks at me. Even lying down, his chin has that defiant tilt.

"Get up and go downstairs." I reach to grab his arm and help him along, but he rolls away onto his feet. His head grazes the rafters. He's tall for fourteen. He takes after the men on my side of the family. Before long he'll have a beard he can braid like his Viking ancestors.

I'd send him out to tramp through the woods on his first hunt if I could track down any of those cousins or uncles who were everywhere when I was growing up. It would be good for him.

"What are we having anyway?"

"Toast."

He raises an eyebrow and makes a face.

"With apricot jam," I say definitively before he can get his complaint out.

I watch as he digs a shirt from the pile and shuffles down the stairs. As I bring up the rear, I glance through the dormer window and notice the trash fire has grown. Thick black smoke billows from the bin.

As I round the landing, there's a knock on the front door.

Little feet scurry.

"Tigis!" the girl cries. The doorknob slams into the wall. A sprinkle of plaster from the hole I need to repair ticks to the wooden floor.

"Don't slam—" I don't even bother finishing my sentence as I hurry across the room and reach for the door to pull it away from the wall. Words circle around and back. They've lost all meaning through repetition. I need a new language.

Tigis steps inside and pushes a pot into my hands. She is the type of woman I would take care never to stand by when I used to go to the club: petite, fragile. Next to her I look hulking. She just barely looks me in the eye, not giving me enough time to decline or be embarrassed. I wish we could be better friends than we are, because she completely understands food stamps don't come for another five days.

She says something I don't understand. I'm not sure what language she speaks. Is Ethiopian a language? I always mean to look it up and check out a dictionary from the library. I'm going to get her something with the tips I earn on my shift tonight. I can't imagine what she might like though.

"Take me with you." The girl clings to Tigis' arm. "I don't want to stay here. Please!" Tigis smiles and strokes my daughter's hair.

"Stop that." I get a bad feeling in the pit of my stomach when the girl says things like this. Nothing is so terribly wrong at our house. The angel isn't a real harbinger of cold to come. The angel isn't real. The angel—

I want to hug the girl and let her know everything is okay, but I have the pot in my hands. There are bits of chicken, and the sauce smells exotically spicy. "Come and eat now."

Tigis says something in her language.

The girl grins like she understands and lets go of the woman's arm. "She says I can come over later."

"We'll see."

I say, "Thank you," to Tigis with a smile. I don't like this secret code she and my daughter share, but I don't want to be rude. The girl is mine. I've given up all of my dreams and possessions to keep her happy.

Tigis turns and walks down the stairs. There's a man huddled into a puffy coat, like he doesn't want anyone to see him waiting at her door.

The last time the girl went downstairs, she came home with ten dollars and fingers smelling like cat pee. Tigis' husband gave it to her for helping put weed in little Ziploc bags. It's just weed, but still. And people I don't like the looks of, like that man in the puffy coat, come and go all the time. It's no place for a kid, a girl. Bad things can happen to girls in the blink of an eye, things they won't ever fully recover from. Maybe there's a chance I can keep her safe just a little longer. At least here there aren't cousins and uncles on the safe side of the locked door.

"Close the door now. Lock it," I say. "Go and sit down."

I follow the girl to the kitchen and place the pot in the center of the Formica table that came with the apartment. It's cool and vintage-looking. It was the reason I took the apartment, even though it's a hundred dollars more than I should spend. I could imagine how my new china would look on it as we all sat around it and talked about our day. It was a mistake, I know now. A hundred dollars is a lot every month.

The girl throws herself in the chair by the window.

The windows of the house next door glitter behind her head. The orange and yellow flickering in the glass is the exact same shade as the Halloween pumpkin on the refrigerator. The fires have taken the place of the blazing sunset. There won't be any dark tonight as the devils cavort.

I place a plastic bowl in front of the girl and ladle chicken stew into it. I haven't been able to get the new china yet.

There's another fire. This one looks like a pile of leaves in the alley. There are a bunch of teenagers gathered around it, throwing trash on to make it blaze higher. Even through the closed window, I hear a crash and the chime of glass sprinkling the ground. I hope this will all be over before the little kids go out tomorrow night. Where are the police anyway?

"I'm not eating this." The girl pushes her bowl away. "It stinks."

"Tigis made that just for you."

"I don't care."

"Then you can just go hungry and take yourself to bed now." Anger surges in me, filling my mouth with words as sharp as broken glass. Why won't she just eat? It's a miracle we have chicken tonight.

"I'm never going to bed again." Her face is screwed up like she's going to cry. Her pigtail has come unbraided and a strand of it trails into the bowl. "There's a monster in the mattress. He has a knife."

"You *are* going to bed." I tip her out of the chair because I don't trust myself to grab her. The sharpness inside me might hurt her.

The girl screams. It's not her best work. She reserves the worst of her screaming for three a.m. The shrill siren of her five-year-old voice conjures up mayhem and murder and rips me from sleep nightly. The boy told her the monsters aren't under the bed or in the closet. They are in the mattress and there is no way to escape them.

If it wasn't for the screaming, I'd admire the brilliance of this little twist to the tale. He has conjured the ultimate horror. No squeezing eyes tight or covering every inch of skin will keep a kid safe from a monster in a mattress.

"Quiet now. Go get ready for bed."

"No!"

For a second I think about slapping her. She earned it. But that will only make things worse.

The pediatrician says she needs consistent discipline, and time-outs are the way to go. It makes sense in theory. I can pick her up and put her in bed. She won't stay. I'll have to hold her there. How is that different from hitting?

"Do you want some toast?" I say instead. I suppose this is about as consistent as I'm going to get tonight.

She bobs her head with much more enthusiasm than heated bread deserves. I put two slices in the toaster and push the lever. "Where is your brother?"

A shadow flickers by the kitchen door. I think I hear a flap of wings. I hesitate only a second until the front door creaks.

I catch the boy with his hand on the doorknob. "Where do you think you're going?" I sound exactly as ineffectual as my own mother did.

"Out," he says.

"No, you are not. Not tonight. Especially not tonight." I don't have time for this argument. I have to be at the restaurant for my shift in an hour and my gas tank is close to empty. "You have homework."

The boy makes a sound like a serpent and stomps down the stairs.

If he goes through the main door out into the night, he'll be lost. He'll become one of the devils of the night, starting fires and smashing windows. I can't let it happen.

"Get back here now." I run after him and grab his arm.

"Get off me." He shakes his arm and gives me a shove.

The sole of my shoe glances off the edge of a stair. I teeter. An inevitable gravity grabs me. I'm falling. It's a loss of control I haven't felt since I was a kid. My knee, my hip, my shoulder hits the face of the stairs. I land in a heap in the foyer. I'm not hurt. I don't think. This isn't the movies, where every tumble down the stairs ends in death.

The boy stomps down the rest of the stairs and steps over me. His face is expressionless. He jerks the front door open and steps out.

The boy is mine. The teenaged brain isn't fully formed. He's made a mistake, an error in judgment. Or is something truly coming unwired and crossed?

"Is that the kind of man you are going to be?" I heard my mother say these words a hundred times. She never did find the language that would deliver the message.

I hear the boy's shoes hit the porch steps. I don't get up right away; instead I stare through the door into the deep violet sky. The air smells of burning plastic, but under it all there's a hint of snow. I'm going to have to find the box with the mittens in it soon. It's somewhere in the attic with the knife and the spiders and the poop in a jar. I'll have to beat back wings to get into the darkest corners, because the cold times are coming.

What am I going to do now? If one wheel falls off, the whole cart collapses. Who's going to take care of the girl tonight? The boy is trouble. Is troubled. The boy— I should find a better place for him, with someone who knows what to do. There might still be a chance to save the girl. I doubt I have the recourse to do this. I doubt I can. I doubt— I don't get to throw one kid under the bus to save the other. It has to be both or neither. That's the rule of mothering, isn't it? That's the only justifiable decision.

I swear I hear a flurry of fluttering wings outside the front door.

The boy peeks his head in, then steps inside. He holds out his hand to help me up. "Sorry, okay?"

"Okay," I reply. I take his hand. It's exactly as cold as the night.

"I..." His face is flushed like he has a fever.

"I said okay." Things are far away from okay, but the word means something specific only to me in the language I speak. "Can you put your sister to bed? I've got to get gas for tonight."

The boy looks at me longer than he has for a while. I think he's disappointed that I didn't hand out a grand punishment. He's just done the worst thing he's done so far. I've been unveiled, revealed as a fraud and a coward. I'm powerless to keep anything intact. I can't stop him from breaking things. I can't stop him from breaking. I can't stop him—

I step out into the night, the gas can and plastic tubing I stash in the foyer in hand. Fires are blazing. It's much worse than it looked from inside. The flames from the eviction heap lick high into the sky, higher than the second story, where the items in the pile once furnished a home.

Devils skulk on stoops or duck into the alley. They carry liquor bottles pre-stuffed with oily rags. They are kids by daylight but something else entirely tonight.

It's too late to sneak into the neighbor's back yard and siphon gas from his old RV with the flat tires. I'll never make it to work on time. Not a chance. It's too bright for that in the firelight anyway. It's too late to continue on this half-baked, ill-conceived plan. It's too late to continue. It's too late—

I stick the hose into the gas tank of my car and it hits some sort of obstacle. This works just fine on the old RV around back. I guess my old beater isn't old and beaten enough. I slump against the hood and stare into the blazing heap of trash next door. I'm out of energy and ideas about what to do next. I'm out of energy. I'm out—

A shadowy figure emerges from the flames. Black wings beat the thick gray smoke until it swirls. The figure resolves into something more ordinary.

"Shouldn't be out here on a night like tonight," Colonel Carpenter says. "Devils will get you." He doffs his hat at me and leans on his cane.

I shrug at him. "I guess," I say. He probably thinks I'm rude. I'm pretty sure he knows I've been stealing the gas from his camper, so rude is the least of it.

"Your boy..."

"What about him?"

"He's running the streets. Making all kinds of noise." The old man's eyes are obscured by the brim of his hat. "I'm going to call the police."

"He's inside." I glance up at the attic window. It's mostly dark, but I'm pretty sure I see the outline of the angel Ariel's wings and the glitter of her eyes as she watches me.

"Last night," the Colonel says. A wisp of his Old Spice cuts through the smell of burning plastic, and then it's gone. "Ripping and running with his boys, then up there." He cocks his thumb to the balcony off my living room. We don't go out on the balcony much, because the railing isn't sturdy.

"Blasting that damn rap music and throwing their empties at cars passing by. Had your little one up there with them knuckleheads."

Of course that happened. Of course it did. Why would I think otherwise?

"I'll talk to him about it," I say. "It won't happen again."

But it will. I can't stop events from unfolding. I can't stop them. I can't—

"You need gas?" the Colonel asks with a nod at my gas can.

"I do." Now more than ever.

"There's a can over there on the side by my mower." He pushes his hat down. "Welcome to it."

"Thank you," I say as he hobbles off to shake his cane at the rest of the neighborhood.

I find the Colonel's mower at the side of his house and just like he said, there's a gas can. As I grab it, a rag snags on the lawnmower gear and pulls loose. Gasoline dribbles from a rusty hole in the can. I'll have to move fast if I'm going to move at all.

Seconds flutter by like years unfurling. The cold times are coming. Worse times. Much worse.

I sprint up the porch steps, then the flight to my apartment. The door knob slams into the wall and plaster ticks to the floor, one more thing I will never repair. I dash through the living room and even step up on the ugly sofa.

The girl's teddy bear, still wearing my gaudy earrings, gives me a glassy-eyed look of disapproval. I run down the hall for good measure, past the girl's room with the knife-wielding monster in the mattress and back again through the kitchen. The pot of chicken stew is congealing into something inedible. I won't forget to return the pot this time.

The pan of cloves and cinnamon sticks has boiled dry again. No need to fill it or worry about it tonight. No spice can mask this smell.

I climb up the last flight of stairs to the attic. I stand at the top and gaze into the shadowy depths. Gasoline drips on my shoes. I didn't think I was gone that long, but I guess I was. The boy and the girl are sleeping. I place the gas can gently on the floor so I won't wake them. It's not so full anymore.

I lie down with them on the filthy black-and-white checkered futon as the devil light flickers along the trail I have made.

The girl snuggles up.

"It's hot in here, Mom," the boy murmurs, not fully awake.

The boy and the girl are mine, forever and always. They are mine to care for and love.

I lie still gazing up into the rafters watching the fire light flicker and the shadow wings beat. I try to recall something pithy my mother might say at moments like this, but language is inadequate to describe how something so hot can be the harbinger of something so cold.

As the air grows thin, I wait for the angel Ariel to descend and cut out my heart, because I can better do my job without it. As the air grows hot, I wait for the angel Ariel. As the air grows hot, I wait—

The Moments Between

— ONE —

I push the root cellar door, and it lands with a thud that stirs up a puff of red dust. I watch it settle for a minute, then scoop up the A&P sack I use to carry the onions, carrots, and potatoes.

"I told you not to go down there," Big John says.

His scratchy voice startles me from my thoughts, which is okay because I don't really want to be thinking them.

I rattle the bag in his direction and tilt my head so he blocks the sharp light from the sun setting over the top of the big mimosa in the way-back of the yard. The rays of the sun spread out around him in a pinwheel of hard yellow light. For a second he's only a dark space where a body should be. It's like he's already gone, but then my eyes adjust.

His red plaid shirt is untucked and hangs on him like a scarecrow. He doesn't eat what I cook anymore. He says he can't work up a taste for it.

He can't work up a taste for much of anything since Baby John passed. Not work, or the girls, or me. Especially me. Neither can I, to tell the truth.

"There's mold spores down there. I told you that."

"That's just not true, John. It's the same root cellar as it always was."

He stares at me hard, like he's seeing someone he's never seen before. "You should have never taken my only son down there and let the mold spores kill him."

The mother always gets blamed, without exception. Doesn't even matter what I say. I ask anyway, because maybe he can tell me the magic incantation that will make everything right again. "What do you want me to say?"

John gives me nothing as he turns away and walks toward the back of the house.

It wasn't mold that killed my baby. I'm sure of that, but there's no way I can make sense of what did.

I put the cement block on the cellar door to keep the wind from catching it and making it bang, and carry the sack to the kitchen to make a dinner nobody wants to eat—

— TWO —

When I pull my car into the driveway after work, I'm in the mood to sit down and prop my feet up, but I have plenty else to do, dinner and laundry and about fifty other things I'm not going to get done. There's a lot more work to do since Big John left. Nobody blames him for leaving. Not everyone is brave. I'm not brave either, but I don't know what else to do.

When I step out of the car, something feels wrong with the air. It's hot but has a heaviness to it, like a storm is coming up. It whistles by my ear. I listen to it rattle the dried seed pods on the mimosa tree for a minute, until the fact that I don't hear the girls smashes into me.

When the other noise rises from the ground, it is how I imagine rocks sound when they grind against each other in an earthquake. It's a growl but also a feeling. The sound is coming from the root cellar. It shakes all through my body.

I run with all I've got, tripping over the cracks in the asphalt but not falling. All the while, I'm remembering when Joelle and Nicky were little, they liked to play in the root cellar with the pill bugs and the candles and the canned goods. They are just fine, I tell myself over and over as though the words will make it so. It's the coolest place around in the summer. They're just fine, just fine, just fine. It wasn't mold from the root cellar that killed Baby John, no matter what Big John says. They are fine.

I almost fall over the cement block that holds the cellar door closed. It's lying at the base of the mimosa tree like someone strong tossed it aside. When I grab the handle, my hands are shaking so hard I can barely hold on, but I manage somehow. I throw open the door.

"What are you doing down there?" I yell at Joelle "What's that noise?"

Joelle's mouth is set in a hard line, the way she used to do when she was little and I made her sit in the corner. She doesn't answer me.

"Don't make me punish you," I say as she walks up the dirt steps. She has a confidence she didn't have before, and a light in her eyes that no punishment can touch.

Nicky smiles and smiles as she climbs up the stairs behind her sister. She looks me right in the eye.

"What was that noise?" I scream at them. "You answer me now. Right now."

Nicky turns her smile on me and says, "I didn't hear a noise." Her voice is changed. It is deep and rumbling, just like the sound from the root cellar.

There'd been a moment when Baby John was warm and pink even when his little chest wasn't rising and falling. It seemed like everything would be easy and fine, but then his lips turned blue, a deep unmistakable blue. The only other time I've been as scared as now was when I saw for myself there was no escaping what happened to Baby John. That's not something a mother can share with anyone else. That's not a thing a mother can admit to. It's not the kind of thing I can tell anyone, not even my own mother. A mother can never be afraid of her own children.

I push all that from my mind and just do what I have to do—

— THREE —

Last winter when Baby John passed, snow was scarce. There'd been just enough for Joelle and Nicky to scrape up sad snowmen with more red dirt and gravel than snow.

But this year the snow is coming down hard and piling up deep. The outside I can see through the dormer window is a field of sparkling white reaching all the way to the end of the earth. It covers up everything that's wrong about the house with a blanket I hope is going to last for a while.

A little while, at least.

Please.

The snow hides the spot where the roof sags and fills in the crack in the driveway. Hides the fact I've been too tired to cut the grass and put up the kids' toys. It covers up the root cellar door completely, so I don't even have to look at it for once.

Sunday late-morning sunshine is pouring in through the upstairs window, icy blue and pristine. The air is scrubbed clean. Icicles on trees made of glass tinkle like bells.

Joelle and Nicky are under the matching patch quilts their grandma sewed for them last Christmas. They look warm and cozy in spite of the wintry draft from the star in the glass with the hole in the center, where one of them threw her elbow into it as I was making them go to bed. Both of those girls have something evil in them. It's proved harder and harder to make them mind. I can only do my best.

Joelle, as usual, has thrashed in the night and torn up the sheet, exposing a corner of bare mattress. I tuck it back into place and adjust her quilt. Nice and cozy. They look so serene and peaceful, lying there without a care in the world anymore.

The other quilt my mom sewed, the third and smallest one, is folded up just so and placed in Baby John's crib. The sight of it makes my throat clench up every single time I see it. But I don't have the heart to throw it out.

It's always the mother's fault. That's what they say anyways, no matter whose fault it actually is. My mom took Joelle and Nicky for a while after Baby John passed, but my mother is older than her years and couldn't handle them for long. Mama was never very good with kids, even her own.

I wish Big John could be here to share this Sunday morning. I loved winter mornings with him, lingering in bed, his warm stale breath, the smell of sleep, the weight of him. He's long gone though. I barely think about him anymore.

The snow makes it so quiet I can hear every little sound in the house. Every creaky floor board, every loose timber in the eaves, every squeaky door hinge. I hear the gurgle of the coffeemaker, the clink of the oven heating. I know the house sounds. But I know the other sound too. Even under the blanket of snow, I can hear the sound from the root cellar. This time I'm ready.

The sound is what a twister makes when it rips through a town. It's the sound of bricks smashing and metal buckling. It's a deep, dark and unnatural sound coming out of the mouths of little girls. And it's rising up from the root cellar and coming this way.

I'm ready.

I am ready.

I pour gasoline on the quilts my mother sewed.

All three of them.

I strike the match—

— FOUR —

The front yard grass that just a week ago was as long and as yellow as hay is this evening charred and dead as dead. The swing set that could have used a coat of paint doesn't need one anymore. The tubes are jumbled and fallen down. A doll that should have never been left out in the snow lies on its side, flattened and melted, its dress brown with mud. A single eye glitters in the violet light from the setting sun.

The clean and beautiful blanket of snow has been ripped away in a rough circle around the blackened spines that used to be the house.

Hoses and boots and gushes of water damped the smoldering remains they found once someone finally noticed the flames and called the fire department. Hours and hours of burning had obscured most of what the house contained. As hard as they sifted through the char and broken beams, they never once thought to look up to the treetops.

In the way-back of the yard, from the highest branches of the mimosa tree still loaded with brown seed pods even in February, the smell of smoke and fire, burned things, is inside me as much as it surrounds me. There's a stiff blackened toast smell in my sweater, a five-day-old coffee scent in my hair. A haze of campfire smoke hovers around me like a halo, making water stream down my cheeks. The taste in my mouth wants to gag me with its sharp insistent sulfur tang, like I'd bit off the heads of some matches and chewed them up.

I don't know if I'll ever get the smell off me. It's probably too late to worry about that. I should have been worried the first time I heard that sound coming from the root cellar. Then worrying might have done some good.

The mother is always to blame. That's what they say anyways. I stare into the black hole of the root cellar with the door burned away. I wanted to destroy it. End it for good, but instead I've opened the gate. Thrown it wide.

I climb down from the tree.

The sound is rumbling and bubbling up from the root cellar like pitch, spreading north south east and west, up down and all the other directions that people haven't discovered yet, to the edges of the burned-up yard and beyond, to the fields of pristine snow-covered land and into the darkening sky.

I know in my heart it won't do any good.

I run anyways—

— FIVE —

They're going to say I'm to blame. Mothers always are, but I have only done what anyone would.

I slide into my seat on the Amtrak. I bought the farthest ticket I could afford. I never even heard the name of the town I chose for a destination. I can't imagine myself there. I can't imagine a time when all the tragedy is behind me. I fear the bad thing from the root cellar will be waiting for me when I reach my destination. For now, for a little while at least, I can let my mind be empty.

For now, I don't have to explain myself or talk at all. I am completely silent. It's best that way. All I have to do is sit in my seat and ride. I don't have to work or care for anyone or pay any bills. I don't have to cut the grass or put up the toys. I don't have to lock up the cellar door to keep my kids safe. All that is behind me.

I'm hanging for a moment. The train's hum lures me into a calm that can never be matched in the place departed or the place yet to come. I'm suspended in this moment between. One foot is lifted, and the other has yet to fall.

I wish it would last forever.

I stare out the window as the sun beats down on the day-old snow and it melts away. Nothing beautiful ever lasts for long. Ratty corn stalks and turned-up sorghum fields stinking of manure fly by the window. Crumbled-down towns and miles and miles of electrical wire loop from pole to pole as the train churns on away from my house, from the burned-up door, from the root cellar.

A lady as old as my mother sits in seat 3D. She probably wishes she'd asked for the window seat. She leans on the arm rest more than she should and looks out my window. She smells of dishwashing soap and dollar store hairspray, which aren't the worst smells ever.

Hour after hour passes. The light fades, leaving a deep blue smear across my window. I don't sleep. I don't want to leave the safety of the train and travel to whatever world sleeping takes me to. I've been to that place too many nights. It's no place I ever want to go again.

The lady next to me snores. Her head tilts at an uncomfortable-looking angle. I think about nudging her so she won't wake up with a crick in her neck, but that's not my business. My legs would be stiff if I moved them. It's easy not to. I just have to sit in my seat and ride. There's not one other single thing I have left to do.

When daylight returns, I'm relieved to see the rusty tractors and dusty strip mall shops flying by as if everything is just as normal as it should be.

The train pulls up to a block of cement with a boxy station building beside it.

The old lady gets stiffly to her feet. She looks at me like she expects me to get up too.

I'm not going to move from the train for any reason. I'm not going to speak.

The lady looks at me with sad knowing eyes. She doesn't know though. There's no way she can.

I watch through the window as passengers shuffle off and walk across the platform to the station. The lady who was sitting next to me is the last one through the door.

Time seems to be moving unnaturally slow. I miss the hum that lets me know I'm suspended between what happened before and what's coming up. I miss it more than I've ever missed anything.

The lady comes back out through the door, carrying a cardboard tray from a restaurant. She's the last one again. She walks stiffly, like my mother used to do when her hip bothered her. She climbs up the steps and onto the train. I lose sight of her.

A whistle blows. The train lurches forward. The wheels rumble under the floor.

I am so relieved I exhale a breath I didn't know I was holding.

The lady makes her way down the aisle, holding the backs of chairs. She's balancing the tray with two take-out coffee cups and something wrapped in waxy tissue paper. She smiles when she sees me.

It's that kind of smile my mama used when she knew already what I was up to. My heart thumps and I grab the arms of my seat.

The lady sits down with an *umph*. She hands me a cup and one of the sandwiches. "Go ahead. You must be hungry."

"Thank you," I say before I realize what I've done.

My mouth hangs open. I've spoken. I've broken the spell. It can find me now.

The woman lowers the tray on the seat in front of her and places her breakfast on it. She turns to me, smiling the wicked smile Nicky wore as she came up from the root cellar that day.

"Do you have any pictures of your kids?" Her voice is deep and full of vibration. Her eyes are as dead as Joelle's, and her skin is as tissue-paper white as dead Baby John's.

The rumble comes up through the rails, through the floor, the seat, and into me.

All kinds of filth come spilling out as words I never intended to say, like cockroaches from a kitchen drawer. I grab whatever I can and hold on. A bad storm is coming, and I don't have a root cellar to go to.

I was sure I had a little more time before the bad thing caught up.

I was wrong—

Poor Me— and Ted

G lory, Glory, Glory. That's about the stupidest name you can give a person like me. But my mom had high hopes, like lots of hard-working folks do. They use fancy names like they're magic spells. As if naming a kid could somehow make it better than it really is. I don't go in for that kind of crap. I named my kid John. Simple. John.

"I know that mess is up here somewhere, Ted. I know it is."

I heave one more of the brown boxes down from where they're piled up and drop it on the floor. It's not so heavy this time. This one must be a box of old clothes, even though it says "kitchen" plain as day on the side of the box.

"Seems like you ought to know which box, Ted, long as you've been up here. You ought to go on and tell me." I laugh about that because Ted never tells. He never does.

I drop the box on the floor, and dust rises up in a puff. It ought to bother me more than it does, with my damn allergies from all the bad air and all, but the dust motes look kinda pretty, like bubbles, the way they float in the light from the dormer window.

"John would have liked how the dust dances around in the light, wouldn't he, Ted? He would've liked that—at least back when he cared about stuff like that, he would have."

I catch the edge of the silver tape and yank it off. Clothes. I was right. Just as I'm about to close the box back up, the smell hits me. Like turning a page in a picture book, one minute you're in a dirty old attic, and the next you fly back in time to when everything in the world was good and smelled like baby lotion and butter cream frosting. I about put my head right in that box.

"Yeah, I know, Ted. It's stupid to cry over spilled milk."

I fight down the burning feeling that's trying to fill up my chest as I tape that box back up extra tight. Maybe that smell will stay in there. Probably not though. Probably it'll be gone next time I come looking for it, just like everything else.

I pull down another box from where it was wedged on top of the chifferobe that used to be in my bedroom. Back when I had a bedroom, and I didn't have to live in one crappy room because that's all I can afford. I nearly topple over with the weight of the box. It lands on the floor with a thud this time. Bingo. I rip it open.

"Come on over here, Ted. I'm going to fix you up real nice so we can go out. You're going to sparkle just like the Fourth of July."

I unbutton Ted's coat, and as I'm fixing him up just right, that feeling like fire starts burning inside my chest again.

"I don't know why you say it's my fault, Ted. Because it's not. I did everything I possibly could for John. Somebody should have helped me. Wasn't like I didn't fucking ask, was it, Ted? I fucking asked people to help John. They didn't listen."

* * *

Union Station is beautiful, probably the most beautiful train station in the world. I walk across the shiny floor polished up like it's Cinderella's ballroom, and past the leather chairs all done up with brass tacks, and look up at the sparkly chandeliers. Union Station is beautiful, but it's only fake beautiful. If I look under those chairs, there'd be wads of old gum. The bathrooms here are just as nasty as the ones at the Greyhound station. Anyone can go into the train station, and everybody knows a place ain't shit if they let everybody in.

I jam a five into the slot of the Metro ticket machine. Five fucking dollars to ride a damn train. That ain't right. Ain't no way that's fair.

"I know, Ted, life ain't fair. Heard that about a million times."

Ted's looking a little ragged. He could use a new jacket. His is getting a little worn out around the middle. But at least he isn't growing out of his clothes. Not like John did. That kid needed something new every week, it seemed like.

I move out onto the platform to wait for the train. People are lining up. The sun glints off their shiny clean hair and polished shoes and the metal decorations on their expensive briefcases or their Gucci bags or whatever the hell kind of bag rich people carry. They all hold their heads that way so their eyes don't see anybody else. Like their thoughts are so important they don't want them to leak out. I hate that shit. Doesn't matter how much your suit or your shoes or your damn haircut cost, you can look somebody in the eye. Say good morning. How are you? It ain't like I'm going to really tell you how I am or anything. I'm not stupid.

"I know they don't care, Ted. You don't have to tell me. I fucking know they don't care."

I don't know when Ted started thinking it was such a good idea to state the obvious. I don't remember him always doing that when John was around. When John was around, Ted was always telling him stories. Stories with morals and happy endings and shit like that. Lot of fucking good that ever did. John wasn't even listening. Especially not after he got himself a new name. How the hell do you shorten a name like John?

The letter "J," what the hell kind of name is that? That's a stupid name. That's just asking for trouble.

The ground rumbles under my feet. For a second it feels like the whole damn train station is coming down. "Wouldn't that be something, Ted? Wouldn't that be something to see?" But it's just the train pulling in. The slick steel train, all shiny and bright like a new can of air freshener, pulls up alongside the platform. Its doors open with a whoosh. I could have felt the cool air-conditioned air if it hadn't been for all those people crowding 'round the doors. They think they're so fucking important. They think every minute of their day is worth a hundred bucks. If I ask them, I know that's what they'll say. That is, if they'll spend a whole minute on me. Fucking people think their time is worth money.

My old boss used to think his time was worth money. He even said that to me when I had to take time off to be with John, or "J" as he made me call him by then. I knew I needed to be at work. I knew that more than my asshole boss did. He could take off work anytime he wanted and go to a resort in the Caribbean or some such shit like that. Not me. I miss one single day, and I'm fucked.

I hang back and wait for everybody to get on the train. I could go up there and push my way in so I can get a good seat, but Ted wouldn't like that. It's better if he doesn't get jostled around too much anyway. When everybody finally sits down, I find a seat by the door. It's all full of newspaper, but at least it doesn't look like a bum pissed on it or anything.

"Save my seat, Ted." I laugh out loud at this, because that's what John used to say before he was "J." Before they shot him in the head. Before he became the kind of kid who goes by the name of "J" and ends up in the wrong place at the wrong time. Always happens. Always does. He was just asking for trouble. Well, he got it, didn't he?

"I'll watch him for you," a little kid says. He plops down in the seat next to Ted.

The kid is maybe seven or eight. His clothes fit him exactly, like his mom didn't ever have any trouble keeping him in clothes that fit. That kid shouldn't be on a train by himself. I look around to see if someone looks like his mother. A kid shouldn't be on the train alone. A kid shouldn't be on the train.

"Not my problem, Ted." The kid has a mother to watch out for him. One of those rich mothers who never have to worry about how their kid will turn out. I did my best, and it didn't do one fucking bit of good. Nothing I can do about it now.

"All right, you watch him," I say to the kid. I put Ted in the kid's lap, and pat his brown furry head. He was a good friend to John. He always was.

I pull my phone out of my pocket as I walk down the aisle and back out the door. It's a cheap phone like you get at the 7/11, but that doesn't matter. It works. It gets the job done.

I step out on the platform and move down a ways as I'm punching in the numbers.

When I punch the last one, the train's doors swish closed. I think about that kid in there with Ted, and how Ted's watching over him, just like he used to watch over John before he was "J." Did that kid's mother ever worry for one minute, one hundred-dollar minute, if she'd be able to keep her kid safe? I doubt it. She doesn't have to. Everything is easy for her.

Fire rises up in my chest and burns like it's going to kill me. What if Ted is right and it really is my fault, all the stuff that happened? That thought makes the fire burn even hotter. I don't worry about that pain, though, because—BLAM!

The blast rattles the platform and shakes Union Station. For an instant, about as long as it takes for a bullet to exit a gun barrel, fly through the air, and blast through my boy's skull, all motion is suspended.

And then, all at once, smoke and fire pour from the twisted metal of the train. Bits of metal, shards of glass, chunks of cement rain down on the passengers' shiny clean hair and polished shoes and expensive briefcases or Gucci bags. They scream, all of them, like they have a fire burning inside.

"Glory, glory, glory, Ted. Now they know what it feels like to be me."

Silent Passenger

The twinge in Jerri-Lynn's eye tooth goes off like a siren, more a sound than a pain.

The suit standing at the break room whiteboard under the unforgiving eye of the LED lights doesn't hear it. Of course, there's no reason he would. Jerri-Lynn knows this on an intellectual level, but the sensation of pain is so present in the world it seems unbelievable that no one else can perceive it.

The suit keeps on talking and pointing with his laser like nothing is wrong. "The neural networks of the processor power the mechanism by pulling energy from objects moving in a co-equal direction." Zip, zip with the laser pointer.

What does that even mean? Jerri-Lynn feels stupid. She suspects the words are chosen for that very purpose. *Neural networks—processor—co-equal.* Technical words, manly slang. She could figure it out if she tried. She'd deciphered the language of trucks. *Solenoid—drivetrain—S-cam.*

It isn't that hard once the top layer is peeled back.

"When objects move in a dis-equal direction, they decrease the efficiency of propulsion by twenty-five percent, thus effectuating a need for additional propulsion—" The suit turns and swirls the laser in front of each of them, as though they might chase it like cats, then finishes with a dramatic flourish, "—i.e., drivers."

Dis-equal—propulsion—effectuating. Jerri-Lynn could look up the words. Ask the questions everyone has but no one is asking. Her heart isn't in it. She doesn't want to learn anything new that she'll never use again after this one last run. She should probably care more, but she's more concerned about the fact that she can't imagine what she's going to do next. The truck will go. With her for a while, then without her.

The suit's way of speaking is hard and clipped, like Italians in movies but with most of the edges filed off. The words he's saying sound practiced. He's not the scientist. He's the pill the scientists want the drivers to swallow. The company probably thinks they'll listen to this thinly-disguised tough guy more than an actual intellectual. The guy isn't from Wichita, yet he doesn't have a speck of insecurity about being an outsider. The opposite, in fact. His confidence fills the room like expensive cologne. Jerri-Lynn wonders what it would feel like to be that sure of herself. It'd be hard to hate anybody more than the flannel-clad good ole boys in the break room hate this dude. Waves of it waft off them. He isn't fazed at all.

Charlie Mason raises his hand the way kids do in school. It's not a thing a grown man usually has to do, and he's got a look on his face like a dog that made a snack out of the trash.

The suit tilts his chin at him.

Charlie shuffles his feet on the cement floor before he says. "Alright, tell me if I'm understanding this correct. We don't stop for gas no more, right?"

"That's right."

"Why's that again?"

The suit's eyes narrow, and he gets a look on his face like he'd whack Charlie with a newspaper if he had one. "You want me to start over from the beginning?"

The guys around the table groan in unison.

Jerri-Lynn feels like groaning herself, but mostly because her tooth is throbbing.

"Nah, don't do that." Charlie takes off his glasses and wipes the lenses on his T-shirt. "I just want to be for sure that I don't have to stop for gas."

"That's right."

Charlie perches his glasses on his nose and squints at the whiteboard.

"Lookit." Bill Pullman grabs a napkin. "You know that joke about how you make a car go by raising up the rear wheels so it's always rolling downhill?"

A few of the guys chuckle, then choke it off when they realize they're laughing at Charlie's expense. Before the new management took over, Pullman never talked much in the break room, being the only black guy on the crew. Seems that times have changed enough that he doesn't have so much to worry about such things anymore.

"Yup," Charlie says.

"It's like that," Pullman says, "only not exactly." He leans back and grabs the marker off the whiteboard tray and scribbles on the napkin. "The trucks get their power from each other and the other vehicles going in the same direction. Like there's a magnet pulling them all along."

The suit comes over and looks at the napkin. He twists his mouth into something like a smile and bobs his head. "Only it's not a magnet."

"Right," Pullman agrees. "Just an analogy."

Jerri-Lynn still doesn't get it. She doesn't really understand why she has to. Men like to know stuff even if it doesn't change a thing.

"Then how come it's different on County 287?" Jerri-Lynn asks. "They don't have the magnets put in yet?"

Pullman gives her an exasperated look.

"There aren't any magnets," the suit snaps like she's said the stupidest thing ever.

She should have kept her mouth shut.

"Yeah, I don't get it either," Charlie says.

Pullman draws a bunch of lines on the napkin. "Because County 287 is two lanes in each direction, and the vehicles going east drag down on the vehicles going west instead of giving them power."

"Yeah, and..." Charlie says.

"It's a bug," Pullman says. "And we got to help the trucks by giving them power to get to the four-lane road."

"Hmmph." Charlie grumbles. "Might as well use gas."

"You bought any gas in a while, pal?" the suit says in his testy way. "Costs as much as the load you're carrying." He turns back to the whiteboard.

"Like solar panels made of people," Pullman says, grinning at his own wit.

Pain is punishment.

Jerri-Lynn isn't sure what she's being punished for. Could be a lot of things. Most likely eating a donut for breakfast one too many days. She wants to get up from the table and get an aspirin or whatever from the drawer under the coffee machine, but she doesn't want to draw attention to herself. Ever since most of the regular crew had gotten laid off, the spotlight has been on her. Everyone thinks she was one of the chosen few for politically correct reasons. She's the only female in the room. And years of experience have taught her never to shine a light on that.

The suit keeps on with his lesson like Pullman didn't even explain it better. When he gets to the part about the IRL beta testing, the thought that saying "in real life" takes exactly as much effort as saying the initials causes another siren of pain to shudder through Jerri-Lynn. This convinces her to get the aspirin anyway. She slides her chair across the floor, rolls her shoulders forward and makes her way as unobtrusively as she can to the medicine drawer.

"Don't leave now," the suit says, flashing a mouthful of brilliant white teeth. "I'm just getting to the part where you get paid to coast."

The guys around the table rub their stubbly chins and chuckle in fake solidarity with the suit, even Pullman who should know better. Jerri-Lynn has a reputation for coasting. There's always rumors like that whenever a woman has a man's job. There's no way the suit would know what the good ole boys say, but it makes the joke richer. Anyway, there's probably some truth to it. She's not adverse to doing things the easy way.

We are all Judases now. No one is any better off than anyone else. Those of us holding on to the tail end of how things used to be, we're worse than scabs ever were. We're not only betraying our fellow drivers, we are species traitors. Laugh harder, sons of bitches. Not long from now, you won't have to complain about women taking what's yours anymore. These machines are going to be the end of us for good. The suit doesn't know it, but it's just a matter of time before they come for him too. We're all fucked. We're all good and fucked.

Jerri-Lynn doesn't feel as bad about the situation as she probably should. It's been a good long time since she's felt anything one way or the other about the state of her life. Now the good ole boys are up the same creek without a paddle. That's okay by her. Misery loves company, as Jim used to say.

She hadn't thought twice about signing on for this job. It had been the right thing to do. She's got bills. She's got plenty of those. It's her only choice, really. Work is the only thing that holds the void at bay.

She should have paid the extra twenty-five dollars per pay period for dental and seen the dentist already. This toothache is going to cost a fortune, and chances are her insurance won't be around after this last run.

She shakes out three pills from the bottle, swallows two, and presses one against the depression in her eye tooth.

"All right," the suit says. "Enough theory. Time to get this party started."

Jerri-Lynn takes a swig of burned coffee from the bottom of the pot, tosses the cup in the trash, and follows the group into the harsh arti-ficial sun of the garage. The truck in her bay looks like any other she's driven lately. She hopes she doesn't have a load of liquor this time. Road bandits seem to be able to sniff that prize out from miles away. If she's hauling liquor, she'll have to take extra precautions to keep from getting herself robbed. That'll mean no rest stops after dark and generally less freedom. No use worrying though, she'll get the manifest soon enough.

She'd like to be on the road already. Sitting idle makes her itchy. All this talk with whiteboards and pointers and interaction with people she'd rather not talk to is exactly the kind of stuff that made her quit her office job and become a driver all those years ago. Jim never liked the idea, but he should have thought about that before enlisting. Jerri-Lynn never liked the idea of him going to some off-the-map mountain in the middle of nowhere to play with guns either. He hadn't listened to her, so she hadn't listened to him. The twinge in her heart reminds her that she once thought fighting Jim was a good idea.

Jerri-Lynn climbs up into the cab. It looks enough like every other truck she's ever driven since she had to sell her own to cover expenses, so she feels confident she can do the job. *Expenses* isn't a word that really covers what she lost... The thought she's doing all she can to hold off the memories sends an ache through her as sharp as the sensation in her tooth. Pain is a reminder. The worst has already come to pass.

She climbs up into the cab, grabs the tablet with the manifest and flicks it on. Liquor, of course.

There's a few odd things in the cab. A rubber nipple that fits on her index finger like a condom, and a strap that goes around her chest. The gear shift is disturbingly simplified. It looks like a Frankenstein switch: down for dead, up for electrified, but other than that, things are the same. Jerri-Lynn straps herself in and rolls down the window.

"Ready to roll!" the suit says with way too much enthusiasm. He weaves through the lineup flashing his bright smile and nodding at the drivers. The artificial light glints off his too-groomed hair, making him seem unreal somehow, as though he too is made of metal and technology.

One after another, doors roll up and the trucks slide out into the pale morning light. Jerri-Lynn grabs the gear shift and drags it into the *electrified* position. No engine rumble rattles the cab, but there's an ever-so-slight tightening in the chest strap. All the dash lights come on to let her know the truck is ready to go. She depresses the floor pedal and the truck glides soundlessly onto the road.

The suit yells some technical gibberish at Jerri-Lynn that she ignores as she turns out of the lot and pulls onto the feeder road to County 287. She's in control of the rig. She was afraid maybe it would steer itself and she'd be at its mercy. That comes later, she thinks bitterly. She accelerates up the access road. No matter how hard she depresses the pedal, the speed gauge won't go above 63.

The morning is sweater cool and the sky is an enormous expanse of cloudless blue, the kind of weather that tricked her into thinking she was going to like Wichita when she and Jim moved into their first apartment by the Air Force base. She'd liked the town back then, but she would have been happy anywhere, in the middle of the desert even, when she and Jim first got married. He was a force in her that weather couldn't touch. With him gone, she's on shaky ground. She feels acutely how much of an outsider she'd managed to remain. In ten years she hadn't gotten to know much about the place at all. Of course, she knows which way the streets go, how to get to the grocery store, what the local TV channels are, but she'd never bothered to make Wichita home. Ten years really flies by.

She's greeted by the sign that lets her know the distance to Lawton, to Childress, to Amarillo, dusty western towns rich in rugged history and lore. Like most places in Texas, they are built for the locals. They hide all their secrets from people just passing through. Amarillo is where the 287 meets the I-40. Amarillo is where the machine takes over and Jerri-Lynn coasts. Two hundred miles or so, and she can coast.

Jerri-Lynn wishes she'd stopped at the Beverly Liquor on the out-skirts of town and picked up two pints from Jorge. Seems almost a crime not to stop in and say good-bye to one of the few people on earth who know her by name on what will probably be her last run. She should have signed up with that other outfit when she had the chance. Too late for regrets now. Hopefully she won't land in a dry county by nightfall. She is going to need something to dull the ache tonight. All the aches. She puts her tongue in the depression in her eye tooth. Sometimes dull-ing the pain is the only option. On an ordinary haul, she'd know exactly how far she could go in a day. With the machine in control, there is no telling where she'll land.

Miles of ranch land littered with pump jacks that don't know they are living in their end times fly by. Jerri-Lynn turns on the radio and pushes *seek* until she lands on a call-in show out of Lawton. The signal won't last long, but she likes getting a peek into the guts of a place. They give up their secrets on these radio shows. She wonders if they know that.

Solitude is the best part of driving. The suspended place between leaving and arriving is a vacation from the job of living. All work is like that, Jerri-Lynn thinks in a moment of clarity. That's why so many peo-ple neglect everything else for it. It's good to have a purpose, if only for a while.

Jerri-Lynn doesn't bother to pass the cars and other trucks. 63 miles per hour is not fast enough to get around any but the oldest jalopy. The throb in her tooth has dulled to the point that it's bearable if not com-fortable. If it was like this all the time, she could probably skip the den-tist.

Pain is a warning.

The pain will be back with a fury, Jerri-Lynn knows. It is just a matter of biting down on some sweet thing or breathing in cold air. That's how pain is. Whether Jerri-Lynn uncovers its true nature and purpose or not, one thing she is sure of, it will definitely be back. Would have been nice if Jim could have figured out that one fact. He'd chased the cure like he was going to put an end to it for good. His persistence was what got him in the end.

Thoughts of Jim threaten to saw into her and slice her open, laying bare all her raw nerves. Gone is gone. It's better to put him out of her mind. She's already thought about every detail of what went wrong for months on top of months and that got her nowhere. *What if he'd talked about the IED that had blown up his friend and irreparably twisted his spine? What if a different doctor had prescribed less dangerous medicine? What if she'd been kinder, or tougher, or different in some way? What if she'd followed him around and discovered what he'd been up to in the months before everything went wrong instead of trusting the lies of a man in the grip of an irresistible pain?* Re-hashing the details never changes a thing. Jerri-Lynn settles into the road hum with its vibration under her feet and lets the rig carry her into the space between leaving and arriving.

The lilt of the Texoma twang punctuated by staccato bursts of home-style swearing about football or Oklahoma City politics buzzes from the radio like an especially docile horsefly, not really annoying enough to do anything about. Jerri-Lynn eats mile after mile of white dashes and stripes without thinking about much of anything. The throb in her tooth flares just enough to keep her from getting comfortable.

"Jerri!"

Jerri-Lynn jumps. The voice slashes through the white noise of her thoughts. Jim's voice. Unmistakable.

"Pull over," Jim's voice demands. It's only his voice, not him. It can't possibly be him. He's gone. Of that one thing she's sure.

She twists her head from side to side. She's alone in the cab. Instinctively she slams her palm into all the radio buttons at once. The talk radio voices fall silent. She grips the wheel, leans into it, listens.

"Pull over."

The voice is impossibly tangible, like a crack of lightning in the middle of the night that blows sleep away. She is compelled to hear it, even though it can't be a real thing. Can't possibly be.

JCT I-40 Amarillo 3 MILES. The sign flashes in front of her eyes.

Impossible. Where had two hundred miles and three hours gone? That is a lot to lose.

The strap around her chest compresses enough for her to notice but not enough to be uncomfortable. It feels disturbingly like a hug.

Alongside the road, a man wearing jeans with the creases ironed in and a thin jacket over a pristine white T-shirt waves her down. He doesn't seem agitated. His motions are controlled, in fact, perfunctory, as though he's been waiting for her.

Jerri-Lynn's heart skips a beat. The strap tries to soothe her with another hug. This man cannot possibly be who he appears to be. He's stepped out of the time where ironed creases in blue jeans were in fashion, a time when a young soldier could believe in things. She's projecting her memories onto the blank canvas of a hitchhiker. That's the only explanation. When she pulls the wheels onto the sandy shoulder, the rubber nipple on her index finger contracts. The rig knows she's decelerating. The rig knows.

Passengers are strictly forbidden. Jerri-Lynn has no doubt this transgression will be thoroughly recorded by all the devices that must surely be standard in a vehicle like this. She's not deterred by half-remembered rules. This is her last run; the rules are unfurling before her like dice tumbling down a craps table.

She rolls to a stop.

Jim's revenant shoulders a duffle bag, runs to the door and pulls it open. A gust of winter air—heavy with the arid scent of scrub wood and the dug earth of gopher burrows, but with top notes of asphalt and exhaust—blows over her. She breathes in the chill of it. The siren of her toothache sounds. He climbs in without asking her destination or any of the usual questions a rider would. In spite of the fact that such things are impossible, it's as though he actually is Jim, and not just the conjured image of the specter who's been riding with her since she found herself all alone. The resemblance is remarkable. Even the smell of him is Jim's.

"Hey," he says when he settles in. He runs his hand over the brush of his close-cropped hair.

The ache in Jerri-Lynn radiates all through her, tainting everything close by.

"I'm taking the I-40 west as far as it goes," Jerri-Lynn says. This is the first time she's thought about her destination. It's a black hole, the future, once this last run is done. A foreign landscape she doesn't have the will to understand. Electronic language is on the verge of rendering her illiterate in a world she once navigated with ease. She'd almost rather go into it blind.

Jim doesn't respond. In every way he's the silent rider by her side.

Jerri-Lynn electrifies the lever, depresses the gas, and the rig pulls onto the highway. The sequence that initiates motion in so many tons of metal is too easy somehow, as if the truck has a will to be in motion and is making things as easy as possible.

"Where are you coming from?" Jerri-Lynn asks as the last few miles of County Road 287 fly by.

The passenger turns, looks at her with his blank canvas face. "It's where I'm going that counts."

He's right about that. Jim is right about that. Jerri-Lynn yearns to believe her man is beside her again. She wants to fall into the dream, but she's afraid to reach out, to touch him. She fears that the tenuous illusion might disintegrate, and she'd find herself touching some random man she found alongside the road.

"Well, where are you going then?"

"I'm going where you're going," Jim says. "Where is it you want to go?"

She pushes the button for the radio. A Waylon song, with a scratch in the same place as her old vinyl copy, conjures up the weight of the down-filled sleeping bag, the crackle of the campfire, the bullfrogs at dusk along the Red River on their first camping trip, floods the cab.

Jim crooks his lopsided smile at her. "I remember that trip like it was yesterday."

"You remember?"

"I remember what you remember."

How is that possible? Jerri-Lynn tenses up like the pain is going to return. She waits for it. There's a saying about things that are too good to be true. She puts her tongue on the indention on her eye tooth and still the pain doesn't come.

"Are you a ghost?" Jerri-Lynn asks. She doesn't really need an answer. Nothing will change if she knows or she doesn't. She should keep her eyes on the road, but that probably doesn't matter either. She stares at Jim, taking in every detail.

The rig gives her a reassuring squeeze as the red white and blue sign for the I-40 turn off sails into view. Jerri-Lynn doesn't need the sign to tell her she's reached the end of the road where she's needed. The wide-open expanses of earth, sky, cow trails, and mesquite brush of the county road veer into a tangle of steel and concrete and asphalt. All that's left for her to do is to steer one last time onto the interstate and hand over the reins to the machine.

"We've come to the place." Jim's voice has a metallic edge.

Jerri-Lynn squints hard at him. She can't decide if she's squinting to see beyond the illusion or if she's squinting to hold it together. She had feared Jim was an illusion, but she's amazed by how much she wants him to be real.

"We don't need you anymore." The voice coming from Jim's mouth resonates and reverberates in a way no human voice can. It's machine-like, but it isn't unkind. "We don't need you, but we gain nothing from your suffering."

"You'll let me have Jim?" Jerri-Lynn's voice quavers. She's never wanted anything more.

Jim grins his cockeyed grin and his eyes flash with the glint of mischief Jerri-Lynn had always loved. "Yes," he says in a voice that's all his.

As the exchange begins, a thrum and a rumble emanate from the guts of the truck. If Jerri-Lynn had been in control of an ordinary rig, she might have pulled over to check out what was going wrong. But she's not in control. She doesn't worry, because whether she understands or not, the outcome remains the same. The sound swells and the vibration of it becomes a solid thing, like the gravity that pushes back on a roller coaster rider. The magnet, if it is a magnet, or maybe it's bugs in the system, pulls and pushes on her from all directions. It feels like bugs inside her, scurrying to get out whatever way they can.

She squeezes Jim's hand and squints to see beyond the illusion of him as the inescapable sound compresses him. She fears he'll become two-dimensional.

The rig travels at a speed Jerri-Lynn can't comprehend. Digital displays on the dash are an indecipherable blur of symbols she's never learned. Through the windshield, the view is a smear, of what she's not sure. The signs and symbols of driving she knows so well have become something entirely different. She's in a foreign land.

At the moment this thought occurs to her, the scene before her shifts. The blur of rushing motion settles. The unbearable thrum becomes birds singing and crickets chirping. Prairie grass waves like it does on a spring day when it's finally warm enough for the creek to set the tadpoles free. Jerri-Lynn knows she's hooked up as a battery to some kind of magnetic future machine, but that's not how it seems at all. She mashes the clutch and downshifts to second. For some inexplicable reason, the pickup she and Jim bought used just after they got married is bumping along a dirt path down to the Red River. She reaches out and takes Jim's hand. It's as warm to the touch as it ever was. "You don't have to feel no pain," Waylon wails from the radio. The only thing she knows for sure is all *her* pain is gone.

Every last bit.

Rules for Love

Minerva, not Minnie, never Minnie, likes to stay on top of things. It's the only way to ensure a good outcome. In the kitchen, for example, the handles of tea cups should all face the same way. The kitchen towels should be folded in thirds, then in half. Not in half, then in half. Never the slovenly way. Following the rules will ensure a good outcome. Making a list is always a good idea. She keeps one on the front of the refrigerator secured with magnets. Not for herself, of course. She knows the rules. But a visitor would need the information.

1. Tea cups—handles pointed out
2. Kitchen towels—folded in thirds, then in half
3. Spices and such—stored alphabetically in matching containers

Minerva arranges the three cushions on her sofa from largest to smallest and finishes up the third pass with the vacuum. She sprinkles the carpet with the last of the perfume she received a year ago, paying special attention to the area around the bedroom door. The scent brings Donald, and the loving look in his eyes when he'd given it to her, into the room. He's a good boyfriend. As good as they get. She tucks the vacuum cleaner away and sits at her writing desk to compose a note. Her desk is arranged just as it should be.

1. Stamps—sticky side down
2. Pens—caps on, never off
3. Mentholated jelly—third cubby from the left

Again, she takes the shiny foil heart from its pink lacy envelope. Again she takes out her red pen. One more time, she stares at the pristine white interior. She must inscribe the card today, Valentine's Day. If not today, when? It's so hard to find just the right words.

Darling Donald, she begins. She likes it. The alliteration is nice. *Dear Donald* would also be an alliteration, but she doesn't want her card to sound like a business letter.

Happy Valentine's Day, Minerva writes.

She studies her tidy handwriting, then opens the bottle of liquid eraser and paints it out. That's not what she wants to say. That sentiment lacks passion. What Minerva lacks in beauty she makes up for with passion.

1. Rich treats poor
2. Rubber meets road
3. Passion beats beauty

Darling Donald,

On this Valentine's Day, I will love you with all my heart and body. I will wrap my limbs around you and thrust you inside the cave of my soul. I will cover you entirely with my wanting, wanton lips and deliver you to ecstasy no man has ever known.

All my love forever and always,

Minerva

That might be a bit poetic, Minerva thinks as she folds the card and stuffs it in the pink envelope. She could have been more explicit, obviously, but passionate doesn't mean vulgar. Men like women to talk dirty, but men don't always get things their way. Donald will be thrilled even though the note isn't nasty. What man wouldn't? It's the thought that counts. The passion. She licks the envelope instead of using the sponge, because that's the type of woman she is. She does work with her tongue. She fans herself. The room has grown suddenly warm.

A knock at the door startles her. Minerva replaces the cap on her pen and tucks it into the drawer. She's not in the mood for a visitor. Not on Valentine's Day.

The knock comes again. "I can see you through the window, Minerva. Don't try pretending you aren't home again."

Minerva turns. Ariadne, from next door, has her lotion-greasy hand up against the front window as she peers in.

Minerva stands and crosses to the door. She pulls it open, but doesn't say hello. She'd like to say "what do you want" or "go to hell," but can't bring herself to say the words.

"Is Donald here?" Ariadne asks, poking her head in and looking around. Her lips are smeared with brilliant red. The shade belongs on a much older woman. Her eyes, as usual, look space-alien large. Some find large eyes attractive on a woman. Minerva doesn't.

"What business do you have with Donald?"

"My garbage disposal is broken. Again." She twists her face in a way some might find cute. Minerva finds it infuriating.

1. Good fences make good neighbors
2. Keep your own house and let others keep theirs
3. Ariadne better keep her mitts off Donald or she's going to be sorry

"He's not available," Minerva says. *Not available to tinker with your drain on a holiday dedicated to love* is what she means, but Ariadne probably infers her meaning from her expression.

Ariadne steps inside without an invitation. "I haven't seen him around much lately. Is everything okay with him?" She crinkles her nose. "What is that smell?"

"Perfume," Minerva says, glad to answer this question and not the other. Donald is just fine and his wellbeing is none of Ariadne's concern.

"Yeah, but that other smell. Did your freezer break?"

"My freezer is in perfect working order." Minerva considers whether she should push Ariadne out and slam the door. She decides this is not the kind of thing she can do.

"Mind if I wait?" Ariadne strides into the room. Her yoga pants cling to her butt in a way men probably find alluring. She plops down on the sofa, disturbing the pillow arrangement. "Donald is the only one who can ever get my garbage disposal to work." Her giggle bubbles up and fills the room like sewage.

A feeling Minerva has only ever felt once before roils through her, causing her to tremble. It's the dark underside of her passion. This fury is made of the same stuff. Minerva fears she might not be able to contain it. That's the danger of being a passionate woman, she supposes. Just before it spills over, she pulls it back. Like a headache passing, Minerva's fury becomes something more manageable.

1. For every passion, there is an opposite and equal passion
2. Any passion which is multiplied by the sum of another is equal to or greater than the original passion
3. It is always time for tea

Minerva makes her way to the kitchen, leaving Ariadne lounging like the lizard she is on the sofa. She puts water on to boil and takes tea cups from the cabinet. She gets milk from the fridge and unwraps a teabag. When she opens the spice cabinet, her eyes fall on the very first jar. *I must get some anise*, she notes.

1. One teabag per cup—never reuse
2. Milk last—never first
3. Only seven grains of arsenic—never more

Minerva watches as the water in the cups turns brown. Once everything has steeped, she carries the tea service to the sofa and puts the tray in front of Ariadne. "One lump or two?" she asks, holding the sugar tongs aloft.

"No sugar for me," of course Ariadne says. "Do you think Donald will be home soon?"

Minerva puts extra sugar in her tea, because the balance of sugar in the world will be off if she doesn't. She mumbles a non-committal response and tries not to watch too intently as Ariadne lifts the teacup to her lips. The woman slurps in an unattractive way, but Minerva doesn't mind one bit. She counts to one hundred, then says, "I find your interest in Donald to be quite inappropriate." The words come with unexpected passion.

Ariadne raises an eyebrow and sets her cup down. It's not entirely empty, but close enough. "What are you talking about?" she says with her mouth, but her eyes say so much more. Her eyes say she can steal Donald away with the pout of her over-red lips and a wiggle of her yoga-toned butt.

Ariadne must think Minerva is stupid. Or maybe she believes Donald prefers her because she is the more attractive woman. Minerva knows that the broken garbage disposal is a ruse. She'd known from the very first time when Donald had spoken with just a touch too much English on the spin. She'd known what they were up to when Donald returned covered in the scent of foul-smelling soap with a significantly reduced interest in her.

A less confident woman might not stand up for herself. A less passionate woman might suspect that a man as handsome and virile as Donald is using her house as a place to stay after losing his job and won't be around for long. Minerva doesn't suffer from such doubts. Donald had said she was all the woman he'd ever need. That is as good as any contract.

Minerva counts to one hundred again. Anticipation sparkles through her, settling deep in her cave of desire, sparking and thrusting more insistently than the one lover she's ever known.

Ariadne's breathing grows ragged.

Minerva's anticipation rises.

"I'm not feeling so great." Ariadne attempts to rise, but she's overcome by a convulsion. She *is* looking a bit unwell. Vomit splatters the table and drips to the carpet.

That'll need a shampoo, Minerva thinks, and a sprinkle of perfume. Perhaps she'll receive a new bottle. Perfume is the perfect Valentine's Day gift.

Ariadne attempts a step toward the door, but her muscles twitch and spasm, then fail her. She gasps, retches, clutches at her throat. She falls. Her red-smeared lips kiss the corner of the table, overturning the tea tray. Her alien eyes grow impossibly large.

They are quite attractive after all, Minerva thinks as the light in them gutters out.

Minerva puts down her cup. Poor Ariadne should have learned to follow the rules. She steps over the subjugated lump of her former neighbor and glides to her desk. A dab of mentholated jelly kills all unpleasant odors. She'll clean up another day. Not on this special day devoted to love. Minerva retrieves her valentine.

As she twists the knob of the bedroom door, she calls out in her most alluring voice, "Donald."

Donald doesn't answer, but Minerva has learned not to expect too much from a man. That's one of her tricks for keeping Donald with her. Minerva tucks the pink lacy envelope under Donald's pillow and swats a fly away. Another and another flit at her face. She can ignore them. Even embrace them. The hum is soothing somehow, a constant. So much less off-putting than when they were in the white, squirming larval stage.

Donald awaits her with rigid anticipation. She undresses and climbs atop him. She slides over his willing and obliging flesh with all the enthusiasm she felt the very first time. His hands are cold, but in no time at all they'll warm to her passion.

"Happy Valentine's Day, darling Donald. Despite your ardent and most eloquent request, Ariadne will not in fact be joining us for a holiday celebration."

1. Love is as good as a contract
2. Passion beats beauty
3. Following the rules will ensure a good outcome

Envy

S eems like a nice airy cottage in Santa Monica would have a hint of sea breeze in the air. Or at the very least, some of the scent from the luxury soaps Amy concocts in her garage-turned-workshop would filter in, but just like last time Celia was here, a heavy chemical smell hangs low in the room as though the house has its own atmosphere, replete with a cloud of noxious pollution.

Amy lounges in an oversized chair. Her cotton-white hair is pricey-salon perfect. Her silk shift and natural-fiber capris, probably from Nordstrom or somewhere like that, seem tailored to her. Her leg, knee wrapped in an Ace bandage, is propped up on the low table. "Sit. I'd offer you something, but I'm in pain today. Excruciating pain." When she grimaces, her over-tanned skin creases at odd angles like crumpled tissue paper.

"I'm sorry. Is there anything I can do?"

Amy prods Celia with her eyes as though she's inspecting her for imperfections. Women like Amy always do that, as if they're the gatekeepers of everyone's fashion choices and muscle tone. Celia ignores it. She likes the jacket she wore today. It's a good solid wardrobe piece, even if it isn't from an expensive designer.

"There's nothing anyone can do."

Something small and brown scurries from under Amy's chair and skitters into the tassels of the rug. Roaches seem unlikely in a house like this, but Celia most certainly saw it. Maybe it was something else. Do the rich have different bugs?

"My doctor is an idiot, obviously." As though her actions are invisible, Amy lowers her leg and grinds the heel of her jeweled sandal on the place where the bug disappeared. She snags a wine goblet with an intricate "A" etched on it and sips golden liquid from it. "Take my advice: Never become a doctor. It's a profession for shysters and sadists."

"No..." Celia sits down on the edge of the sofa and pulls her laptop out of her bag. Not medicine. Graduate school probably, or maybe she'll give Y-combinator a try. A tech start-up, that'd be awesome.

A loud thump of a door hitting a wall comes from the back of the house. A man with salt and pepper hair steps out into the opening that's part library and part dining room, carrying a small table that looks like it belongs next to a bed. "This one's going with me. I left yours in there." He sets it down by the back door and grabs a yellow can from under the sink.

"Ignore him," Amy says with a twist to her expression that might be due to the pain in her knee. "That's just Charles. He's on his way out. And taking the furniture with him, apparently." She glares in the direction of the husband Celia has heard of but never seen. "Stop spraying that in here. You know it gives me migraines."

"Seeing me with any semblance of peace of mind is the only thing that ever gives you migraines." Charles raises his voice as he yanks out the drawer of the bedside table and coats the inside with bug spray. He taps it on the door frame and dead bugs fall to the white tile floor.

"Leave it," Amy calls out as he reaches for a copper dustpan and brush on a hook. "Same as you leave everything else."

Celia shifts in her seat. The awkward sensation of intruding on a private moment crawls over her and wraps around like humidity. Would Amy care if she left? Does she want her to?

Charles pauses with his hand in the air. "I will then."

"Good," Amy says. "Good riddance."

Charles shoves the drawer back into place, snatches the table up, and slams the door behind him.

Celia sits frozen, unsure of what to say.

"You know, you could do something for me, now that I think about it," Amy says, as though nothing out of the ordinary had happened. "My medication is on the counter."

"Sure."

Celia sets her laptop aside and walks to the open kitchen. A cluster of dead roaches mars the pristine white of the floor. One struggles to right itself and spins in a drunken circle. She scans the counters. Everything is sparse and uncluttered. Her own kitchen always has a soaking pot in need of scrubbing, crumbs on the counters, photos on the fridge. Celia tells herself she prefers things her way as a roach skitters across the counter and disappears behind a cutting board. *At least I don't have roaches.*

"Next to the sink," Amy calls out.

Celia spies the amber pill bottle. Out the window, framed by a lattice of lemon tree leaves and little white blossoms, Charles stacks the table onto the bed of an oversized pickup like he's playing a giant game of Tetris. The truck is loaded with brown packing cartons and miscellaneous household items. He's actually moving out right this moment. Poor Amy.

Vicodin, ten milligrams, Celia reads the label on the pill bottle. Her aunt used to take that when she had her hip replacement. Amy must be in serious pain. She got the prescription for the strong pills that doctors hardly ever give out. Celia turns on the tap to let it run cold.

"Don't bother with that," Amy says.

Celia returns to the front of the house and hands the medicine to Amy. The older woman's lipstick is such a dark shade of red it's almost brown. It's just the shade Celia's been trying to find. She considers whether to ask Amy where she got it, but decides against it. It would likely be out of her price range.

Amy pops off the top and shakes three pills into her palm. She puts them in her mouth and downs them with a swig from her wine glass.

Celia hesitates before picking up her laptop. She opens her mouth to say something, then doesn't. Amy must know the dangers of mixing strong painkillers with alcohol.

"Don't look at me like that." Amy smiles. "These things barely even work anymore."

"Oh, I wasn't..." Celia smiles and sinks into the sofa. She's here to work, not hand out advice. Sharing her thoughts will only jeopardize this well-paid side job and probably cost her Amy's recommendation.

"I've been meaning to ask you," Amy says, "do you know someone who could get me more of these?" She shakes the pill bottle. The rattle sounds like she's got very few left.

"What? No," Celia stutters. "Why would I?"

"Of course you don't." Amy smiles in a wan disinterested way. "But you must have a cousin or something, your people are from *the hood*, aren't they?"

Celia opens her mouth to speak, but words don't come out.

"Don't look at me like that. That's a thing people say, *the hood*."

It *is* a thing people say. Just not people like her.

"You should see your doctor," Celia says with clipped tones, as she tries to decide if this is going to be the bridge she dies on.

Amy rolls her eyes and settles deeper into her chair. "Like I said on the phone," she continues, as though she didn't just spew a gob of racism in Celia's face, "I screwed everything up. With the website, I mean, obviously."

Celia perches her laptop on the squishy arm of the leather sofa and opens the dashboard. Amy has indeed screwed everything up. This would be easier at a table, but it doesn't seem right to ask her to move. "I wrote the blog posts you requested for the new autumn soaps."

"Of course you did." Amy seems distracted.

The chemical odor is less noticeable after being in the room for a while. It's still a mystery. In Amy's house every little vase or candlestick is placed just so, and the fresh flowers are always one-day fresh, and every speck of dust is wiped away the moment it lands. Not by Amy, of course, but the housekeeping she oversees is meticulous in that annoying way that women are meticulous to prove they're better than everyone else. Celia realizes that thought is nine layers down and absolutely not something Amy would be aware of. She's not the self-reflective sort.

"Right? It's a mess, isn't it?" Amy asks. "I'm a techno-illiterate. You can fix it though."

"Of course," Celia says. "What was it you were trying to do? Maybe I can show—"

"I've got more to worry about than all the buttons and such on the internet." Amy waves the idea away. A shadow crosses her face. "You saw him." She looks toward the back of the house as though Charles is still there. "He's quitting his job. Going on a *road trip*." The words drip from Amy's tongue like something bad-tasting she's trying to spit out. "He's made new friends. Young friends he met on Venice Beach. Your people. Not that there's anything wrong with that. Or maybe they're Afro-American, or whatever they want to be called now."

Celia gets the frosty feeling in her chest she always gets when white women push her aside. This comment is just too much. She should say something, stand up for herself and explain to Amy how much micro-aggressions hurt.

"It's humiliating. That's what it is. I'll bet dollars to donuts one of those new friends is a woman. The old horndog. He thinks I'm going to sell the house, which I am most definitely not. A bug must have gotten in his brain."

"Are you okay?" Celia can't help asking, even though she knows the smart thing to do is stay out of it.

"Me?" Amy puts her hand with the perfectly sculpted nails to her chest in a mid-century theatrical flourish. "I'm fine. I've got more to worry about than that idiot."

Celia taps the keys and without much problem reinstalls the template Amy has turned off. All the customizations are intact. It's almost as if Amy knew just what she was doing. The thought that Amy faked this problem to get Celia to come over tickles the back of her mind, but Amy must have friends she can talk to, a therapist at least.

"I'm going to have to sell twice as much soap," Amy says. "With that ass out of the picture, this business is going to have to generate more." Amy sighs in that defeated way that's supposed to generate sympathy but never does, not when someone like Amy does it. "Money always sullies the beauty of art."

Celia smiles in sympathy, even though she's not sure there's much art involved with Amy's designer soaps. They're all pretty standard.

"Wine o'clock," Amy says. She drops her feet lightly to the floor and glides across the room to the bar.

That's supposed to be funny every time, so Celia laughs politely.

"Did you see my rose bushes when you came in?" Amy asks as she returns to her chair. She presses a glass of wine on Celia, who accepts even though she doesn't drink wine.

"Umm...no."

"Drink that," Amy says as Celia leans to place her glass on the table.

Startled by Amy's sharp tone, Celia nudges her bag and her lipstick tumbles to the floor. She tries to catch it with her shoe, although maybe what she really wants to do is hide it so Amy won't judge her for wearing drugstore cosmetics, but it rolls out of sight. Ugh, she should get down and look for it.

Celia takes a sip as Amy stands over her like she's supervising or something. The wine is bitter. The fumes wafting off of it remind her of the chemical odor in the house. For some reason there's a hint of grittiness in her teeth. Celia tries to drink more, but just can't.

"It's bugs," Amy says, with a disapproving scowl that doesn't change her expression much. "They've eaten my bushes like they were salad. Bugs are the bane of my existence. What do you know about that?"

Celia reaches down and feels around for her lipstick without luck. "I don't know, bugs?" Celia says. "Bugs are..." Celia can't decide how to complete the sentence. Bad, obviously. She's not paid to spout platitudes. She's paid rather well to run a website, and she wishes Amy would just be quiet for a minute and let her do it.

"Here." Amy bends stiffly and holds herself up with the coffee table. She reaches under the sofa.

"I'll get it," Celia protests.

Using her sculpted nails as tweezers, Amy pulls out an object made of corn husks and scraps of fabric. She dangles the thing in front of Celia, then drops it on the glass-topped table. "What do you think of that?"

The corn husks are tied with jute rope to form a crude doll shape. Rusty safety pins hold scraps of fabric in a semblance of a dress. The husks themselves crawl with tiny black mites. From under the tattered edge of the skirt, approximately where the vagina would be, a pair of roach tentacles wave.

"Eww." Celia leans back. "What is it?"

"You know what it is. Of course you do."

"Is it... I don't know..."

A roach scurries out from under the doll's skirt, skitters across the table and falls to the floor with a "tic." Amy straightens up, stomps across the room to the bug and squashes it with her toe.

Celia decides she never really liked that shade of lipstick, and there's no way she's ever going to look under the sofa.

"You're not afraid of that?" Amy asks, pointing a manicured talon at the doll. She squints at Celia, as if trying to detect some symptom of her fear.

Amy's leaving the realm of merely eccentric and veering into stranger territory. Celia riffles through her mental note cards, trying to come up with a good excuse to leave.

"Why would I be?"

Amy's scowl deepens. "You're Catholic, aren't you?"

Celia draws in a quick breath. "I used to be—"

"Your people mix up saints with voodoo and cast spells to do people harm, right? Santa-something." She pokes at the doll. "I figured if it will get rid of people, it'll get rid of bugs."

Anger bubbles up in Celia. She can feel it flushing her cheeks and struggling to come out as an angry retort. "Santeria is a religion. It's a form of worship. It doesn't exist so old white people can cast spells to rid their homes of vermin."

That's it. There goes the job. Celia closes her laptop and stuffs it in her bag. She'll have to hustle to find something else. She can do it if she works at it. This isn't the worst thing that could happen. She does the mental math about how hard it will be to pay rent without the five hundred a month from Amy.

"Doesn't work anyway," Amy says, as though Celia's words hadn't registered.

Relief washes over Celia. Even though she should repeat what she'd said and make sure Amy understands, she can't help feeling happy about the reprieve. In spite of her angry words, and even though she meant every one, she's apparently not fired.

"And I've had enough." Amy stalks across the floor, her sandals slapping. "I'm done pussyfooting around." Amy grinds her shoe for emphasis. "They've infested my home, eaten my roses, and one crawled in Charles' ear and turned him into an impostor."

"What are you going to do?" Celia asks.

Seems like an exterminator would be the best solution to Amy's problems. Maybe a little marriage counseling, or a stint in drug and alcohol rehab.

Celia slips the strap of her laptop bag onto her shoulder and stands up to go, still not quite sure what her excuse will be. Better to reschedule for a time when Amy isn't so agitated.

"That's the question, isn't it?" Amy says. "I'm going to grab the bull by the horns and solve this problem once and for all." Amy looks Celia straight in the eyes, almost like she's daring her to try to stop her. "And I need you to drive me so I can get some better supplies."

* * *

Amy marches up and down the narrow aisles, perusing the offerings with a scowl on her face like she's shopping at Whole Foods.

Celia hangs back, taking in the colors of the glossy statues and jar candles. The faintly grassy smell of the place reminds her of when she used to visit the corner store with her aunt to get ginger and lemon grass for tea to cure stomach aches. That was a different time, and this shop seems like it belongs in that long-ago past.

"Where are the spells to get rid of curses? A bug curse," Amy calls out to the plump grandmotherly woman behind the counter.

Celia cringes and opens her mouth to apologize.

The woman smiles like she deals with people like Amy all the time and steps out from behind the counter. She takes a yellow box from the shelf and presents it to Amy.

Amy's scowl deepens as she stares at the package. "Celia, come over here and read this."

Celia weaves around the stand holding packaged roots and herbs, and makes her way down the aisle. She takes the box from Amy. "Chalk de China," she reads. "Kills roaches. It's supposedly very strong."

"Ugh. You know that's not what I mean." Amy sets her lips in a determined line. "Tell her I want something to get rid of a curse. Something really strong."

Celia should have left when she had the chance. She must have been crazy to take Amy on this ill-conceived road trip. "You can't just walk in and ask for magic. It's like walking into church and asking the priest to get God to smite your enemies."

"I'll pay whatever it costs." Amy frowns in that way she does when she doesn't like a change to her website. "Go ahead. Tell her."

Celia stiffens and lets a stream of apologies fall from her mouth before she explains to the woman what Amy wants.

"Don't worry. I've met her kind," the woman replies in Spanish. "We'll charge her plenty for the trouble," she says with a wink that Amy doesn't see.

The woman gathers a selection of roots, a black candle in the shape of a penis, a bundle of dressmaking pins tied with red thread, and a statue of Santa Muerte with an especially gruesome sneer on her skeletal face onto the counter. She explains the steps Amy should take as Cecilia translates.

"Okay, I'll take it," Amy says, pulling out her wallet.

"Five hundred dollars," the woman behind the counter says.

A tiny, almost inaudible gasp escapes from Celia, but she catches herself before saying anything. Amy deserves it for every backhanded insult. She absolutely deserves it.

The woman doesn't flinch.

Amy doesn't even hesitate. She pulls out her credit card and hands it over.

The machine hums and beeps as the woman processes Amy's items.

"Oh, wait." Amy turns and grabs two boxes of the Chalk de China. "These too."

*　*　*

The afternoon sun glitters and sparkles in the tiny Pacific waves as Celia drives Amy's BMW back to her house. The car is so shiny new and high-end it barely seems in the same category as the fifteen-year-old thing she drives.

White privilege is embarrassing even if the things are nice, Celia ponders as she sinks down in the plush seat, hoping no one she knows sees her. She feels like a pretender or a servant, which has some truth to it.

"I envy you," Amy says.

In the bright sunlight streaming in, Celia notices for the first time how tight Amy's skin is pulled over her bones and how deep the creases are that feather her lips. "Me?"

Amy places the brown bag from the botanica in her lap. She takes out the packets of roots and examines them.

"Yes, you." She laughs the way old bitter women do. It's an ugly sound Celia had never noticed before. "You have your whole life spread out like a banquet. You're one of the special ones. The amazing brown girls."

Oh God, here it comes. Celia grips the steering wheel and hopes it will all be over soon.

Amy takes out the yellow box of Chalk de China and opens it. "You get to be smart instead of relying on how toned your thighs are."

Celia's instinct is to stop the car, get out and walk home, but she doesn't. This old white woman is not going to shame her. Still, she becomes hypersensitive to how much space her hips take up in the seat.

"Don't be upset. Your thighs are your thighs." Amy takes out a stick of the pesticide chalk and scratches the end of it with her nail. White powder crumbles into a crease of the paper bag. "The size and shape of your body isn't important to you. That's what I admire."

"What does that even mean?" Celia feels her cheeks and her chest getting warm again. She glances at the growing pile of roach chalk. "You should be careful with that stuff. That stuff isn't even legal, it's so strong. I read an article about it."

"Your intellect can expand to the end of the universe," Amy says, still scratching with her over-long nails at the stick of chalk. "A body can only ever be so good. Just like you can only get so naked. After that there's nowhere to go."

"I guess." Celia wishes she had coffee or something. The drive or the company probably is making her tired. Her throat feels scratchy, like her allergies are coming on.

Amy picks at the stick of chalk, and flakes of powder fall like fake snow into her lap.

"That stuff is really strong," Celia says even though the words she says don't seem to register with Amy. "Maybe you don't want to get it on your skin."

Amy looks up while continuing to crumble the chalk. "Women like you are going to do things and see things and change things. You're going to excel where I only ever treaded water. I envy that, wish I'd been born you instead of me."

"Umm..." For an instant Celia gets a peek through a window where the curtains had always been drawn.

"Even your thoughts are beautiful, pristine," Amy continues. "My thoughts are wrong. Ugly. I hear them. I see how they hit people, but I don't have any others."

"It's not too late..."

"It's entirely too late. I'm an invisible old woman who's lost all her power."

"I'm sorry." For the first time Celia genuinely does have sympathy for Amy, in spite of all the insults and aggressions, or maybe because of them. She's an old woman who doesn't know any better. Amy's right to envy Celia. From Amy's perspective, Celia's prospects do look pretty good. She's got nothing to worry about.

Celia signals, slows, and turns the car into Amy's driveway.

"Nothing you have to be sorry for."

The stick of chalk had become an anthill of white powder. Amy lifts the paper bag carefully, as though she doesn't want to spill a single grain.

As the sun glitters and sparkles on the Pacific Ocean and streams through the windows on a beautiful Santa Monica day, Celia can't stop staring at how the crimson lipstick Amy wears, so red it's almost brown, the color she's been searching for, bleeds into the creases around her lips as she puckers and blows.

*　*　*

First Celia sees the rafters. She can't place them in space. She can't quite understand why she's lying down and looking up.

Next, she hears the clatter of something hard against something harder. The sound is familiar. A beer cooler at a party. Ice, the hard thing is ice. The harder thing is a ceramic tub. It's the tub Amy uses to render fat for her soap. It doesn't feel oily like it should. The rafters belong to the ceiling of the garage-turned-workshop where Amy makes her soap.

Freezing water laps around Celia as the chill soaks into her along with the sound.

Finally she smells the coppery tang of blood. There's a blade that should be cold but isn't any colder than the ice all around her. It's pressed into her skin, sliding through her skin, slitting it apart in the autopsy T-shape that Celia has only ever seen on crime shows on TV.

Ropes hold Celia's arms and legs in place. They're so tight she can't thrash or even move.

"Oh dear," Amy says. "You've woken up. That's unfortunate."

Celia opens her mouth wide to scream. "What..."

"This must be so confusing," Amy says with grandmotherly concern she's never shown before. She slips her long fingernail under the flap of skin on Celia's chest.

A damp sucking noise reminds Celia of stripping fat from raw chickens in her aunt's kitchen, but the facts don't fit. They're not in a kitchen. The facts don't make sense.

And then they do.

Amy slips her hand inside the incision. Amy's motions are calm, methodical, expert and practiced, as though she's trimming her bangs or taking a bath or doing some mundane task that brings her mundane pleasure. She slides first one hand, then the other, under Celia's skin. Farther and farther she reaches, going impossibly deep, separating Celia from herself, peeling the skin from the meat.

Celia doesn't respond. Can't respond, she realizes, because the part of her that she uses for speech has been cut away already.

"Time for my new carapace," Amy says with a warm smile on her tattered and wrinkled old face. Her lips, wearing the perfect shade of lipstick so crimson it's almost brown, are disturbingly close to Celia's face. "I do so envy yours."

Accidental Doors

Out back by the koi pond, where the branches of the mulberry tree have become so overgrown that the shade from it obscures everything, Delanie waits. For what, she's not sure. The sun to set? Now that would be something shocking and new. The sunset is the highlight of most of her days lately. While she waits, her eyes wander along the brick path that leads out of her back garden and stumble on the one wonky brick. Someone should fix that before an accident happens. She sips on a glass of 2014 Alexander Valley Cabernet at $185 a bottle. The good stuff.

Things were so much more interesting years ago. She's not sure what happened. Old people always told her that life contracts with age. She never believed it would happen to her. How did her world get so small while she wasn't looking?

Yvonne, like always, sits like a lump and cracks the ice from her Pepsi Lime between her teeth. It's not much later than 7 pm on this very ordinary Tuesday, and Delanie is so bored she could murder someone. Anything would be better than listening to Yvonne drone on as though no one ever told her that vocal inflection is a thing people appreciate.

Also, "sipping" might not adequately describe how she's imbibing her beverage.

"This year is going to end up being our best ever."

"That's wonderful." Those are the words Delanie drags out of herself. Oh, what she would she give for some stimulating conversation. Whatever happened to nineteenth-century salon culture? Where were the people who traded witty *bon mots* and solved the world's problems with diagrams on cocktail napkins and on the nubile asses of lovely young things? Delanie was born in the wrong century obviously. At least the modern world still produces a decent vintage to take the edge off.

The wind stirs the leaves of the mulberry tree and a single leaf breaks away and falls onto the surface of the koi pond. It floats there like a ship on a stormy sea.

"The wind is coming up," Yvonne says, licking her finger and holding it up. "Santa Ana's on the way." She unzips her waist pouch and pulls out an asthma inhaler. "Always makes my allergies act up."

Delanie ignores Yvonne's inane weather comment. Sometimes she regrets renting Yvonne her spare bedroom. She should have chosen someone more like herself. Someone who appreciates life's finer things and doesn't strap pouches around her already lumpy middle.

Yvonne grins with half of her mouth in a way that Delanie finds especially unattractive. Has the woman never looked in a mirror at her own smile? "We're on track for 8.5."

Delanie ponders the sound that just spilled from Yvonne's mouth. It's a lot like the gibberish she usually spouts, but somehow more significant.

"8.5 what?"

Yvonne cracks an especially large piece of ice and crunches it to bits before answering. "8.5 mil."

"Are you saying the jewelry business is worth eight and a half million dollars?"

Of course they were successful, why wouldn't they be? Delanie's designs are stunning. But hearing the number makes her think she should have been keeping closer track of the paperwork.

"Yup. Looks that way."

Oh, the adventures she'll have and the new things she'll buy. She's always surrounded herself with the affectations of wealth, but now she has the real thing. Could this possibly be true?

"We're millionaires?" Delanie struggles to keep her voice properly modulated. She's always loved beautiful things and beautiful places. And most of all, beautiful people.

"We are." Yvonne guffaws so hard she snorts. She tucks her inhaler away and takes out a stick of silver-wrapped gum. As she unwraps it a sweet fruity vomit-like scent wafts through the air.

"I can buy a place in Palm Springs? Cruise around the world if I want? See every wonder of the world?"

"Oh no. Not yet." Yvonne frowns. Her midwestern accent makes her proclamation all that much more dour. "We're going to re-invest it all into the business."

Oh, but we are *not*. Life is short, and with her barely noticing, it's grown shorter than Delanie would like. She's going to spend this money on an adventure to rival any in all of history.

"We should cash it all out and do something marvelous. We could go on a cruise. Hell, we could buy our own ship and invite every person we ever wanted to meet."

Yvonne laughs like Delanie is kidding. "In ten years we'll be set for life," she says as she winds up her drugstore Chapstick and applies it to the O of her mouth.

In ten years we'll be dead. Delanie's mortality hovers closer to earth than it ever has before. Now is the time for adventure. Now is her very last chance.

"I want my half. The business is based on my designs."

Yvonne crunches and crunches, looking at Delanie with one eye squinted shut. "No. I built this model. It's just now getting started. We're not going to cash out until we've achieved maximum profitability. No."

Delanie gets up from the lounge chair. The blue light glitters up from the bottom of the koi pond. Yvonne is right about one thing. The Santa Anas have definitely arrived. The wind musses her hair as she makes her way to the kitchen to refill her glass. Off in the distance a coyote howls, and another answers. They've found some small creature that will sustain them. The beasts know. The beasts know they need the excitement of the kill to live life to the fullest.

Delanie has always wanted to do something extraordinary. Always. She fears it might be too late already, but if this is her very last chance, she's not going to let it go by. She fills her wine glass, then downs it all to fortify herself. As she returns to the koi pond, she stoops and picks up the brick from the footpath that has never fit as it should.

Yvonne's head, with the horrendously out-of-date haircut, peeks over the top of the bench like a mushroom in the forest. Delanie smashes the brick into her crown again and again and again until it cracks like an egg in a cup. The coyotes howl their delight as the wind picks up and whips the mulberry into a frenzied dance.

At the Vons on Coyote Canyon, an egg falls to the vinyl tile floor and cracks open. The blood in the yolk surrounds a malformed fetal chicken. It looks disturbingly like the contents of the human skull. Except for the unborn baby chicken, of course.

Delanie maneuvers her cart as far away from the mess as possible, brushing close to the wall of cheeses and various flavors of mixers for coffee. She averts her eyes as though this ominous portend has no relationship to her. She pretends she knows nothing about who was examining the carton of brown eggs for cracks.

Over the intercom a young woman calls for a cleanup in dairy, as though this is a small problem that can be solved with a mop and a few paper towels. It's too early for the general alert. How do the authorities know already? Delanie turns her head in response to a squeak, squeak of rubber-soled shoes coming down the cereal aisle.

A man dressed as store manager in a crisp white shirt walks her way with purpose. He's an unlikely candidate for management. Too young, too swarthy, too hardened-looking. He's probably an undercover cop. Delanie's heart pounds. She's not sure she can run fast enough to escape. Of course the authorities are onto her by now. How could she have been so arrogant to think she'd get away with her crime? She takes a deep breath and prepares herself for prison life.

In the time since the accident took poor Yvonne out of the picture, blips have begun appearing in her perception. It's in the space between what one eye sees and the other doesn't. Somehow there's too much space between the thing she's looking at and the new thing she wants to see. There's a door of sorts, a gap where objects and sounds and time don't work as they should. Delanie thinks of these as "accidental doors." Although she's not entirely sure how every aspect works, she suspects they offer her a second chance to correct things that she's done wrong.

Lately, the doors are all over the place. They couldn't have appeared at a better time. Delanie is definitely in need of a second chance. The doors are useful, or will be once Delanie gets the knack of how they work, but they're disconcerting to say the least. There's no controlling them, and she fears people are starting to notice. The going in and out of the world is putting a strain on her credibility and undermining her authority. The last thing Delanie is going to allow is people to treat her like someone's doddering old grandma.

Even though Delanie has pledged to ignore doors when she's out and about, a door forms between the egg on the floor and the manager in the cereal aisle. A crack as sharp as a gunshot transforms the refrigerated air of the grocery store into the hot breath of a Santa Ana, and she's pulled in.

Leaves swirl around Delanie's feet, and specks of debris that have gathered on the canopy of the overgrown mulberry tree sting her cheeks. The old tree, not native to the region but living on this plot of land longer than she has, groans and sways. If it comes down in the wind, it will take out her roof and maybe one more. She's going to get it trimmed back come spring. She's going to fix everything up. But for now, she's glad for its dense canopy that nearly touches the ground. As much as she hates how the tree kills all the other plants in its sphere, she welcomes its camouflage now.

Delanie wields her shovel in spite of the weather. There's no time to waste. She has to take advantage of the dark. This time she's not going to make the same mistake. The hole has to be deeper. Much deeper, so the coyotes won't come. She needs to hurry but not so much she makes mistakes. The roots are tangled and run deep but she won't be deterred by some stupid tree. Delanie digs.

"Ma'am?" the undercover cop says.

His expression is only mildly concerned. Why hasn't he put handcuffs on her yet? Sweat trickles down Delanie's neck. Her body is betraying her. *Stay calm*, she tells herself. *Just stay calm. Prison will be a fascinating experience.*

"Ma'am, is everything okay?" the man repeats. If his expression is any indication, he's more annoyed than concerned.

"Yes, of course," Delanie replies. Just in case he's not in fact an undercover cop on the tail of a master criminal, she scowls at him to let him know she's not the type of old lady who likes to be interfered with. He takes her answer at face value and moves on down the aisle.

Delanie must confess she's a bit ambivalent about his behavior. She is, after all, a murderer on the loose. She could be a danger to society. She *is* a danger to society, and yet all anyone sees is someone's harmless grandma. Delanie is beginning to think she could open fire with a machine gun and take out half the store before the police arrived to blame it on some hapless black teen.

And yet, even though she's owed a measure of fame and notoriety she's been denied, she would very much like to escape detection and run away to another country with more money than the Kennedys. That would be a much better outcome. She ought to keep her head down and just do what she has to do to get all the ducks in a row. Ambivalence.

Even though she knows it might give her away, she can't resist glancing back at the broken egg. The floor is pristine and sparkling, as though no bloody yoke has ever tarnished its shine. This is not the way things are supposed to work.

Damn doors.

Delanie pushes her cart with renewed purpose to the aisle with cleaning supplies. She's used every type of soap in her cabinet without the desired results. She throws a bottle of bleach, some heavy-weight towels, and rubber gloves in her cart. These items huddle together suspiciously in the corner of the basket. The left front wheel has taken to squealing like a misbehaving toddler. Better not tempt fate. She turns the corner to the next aisle and tosses a bar of cooking chocolate, some muffin papers, and a bag of sugar into her cart. For good measure she adds a package of sprinkles, plain, nothing fancy. Now the contents of her cart look far less sinister.

On her way to the register she pauses at a table laden with cupcakes left over from the most recent holiday. Any sensible person would buy cupcakes instead of making a mess in the kitchen, or better yet visit a nice French bakery and pick up a confection actually worth eating. But no one is going to think like that. It's perfectly natural for an old woman to bake. Delanie has grown into the perfect disguise.

There's a song playing that Delanie used to like not all that long ago. Offspring, maybe, or Nirvana. It's not grocery store music. This version is a copy of a copy of a copy, barely recognizable. It *is* that one song she always liked. She's sure of it, but it's so distorted she's afraid to look up because it sounds just like it's coming through a door. She examines the minor holiday cupcake rejects until the next song comes on.

No door appears.

Delanie tucks her purchases into the trunk of the Taurus she plans to replace with something sleek and new and slides into the driver's seat. She tucks the hundred dollars in $20s she got in cash advance into the glove box, with the other $500 she's managed to collect so far. No one even blinked when she signed the name on the electronic display. Why would they? She doesn't look like someone who would use another person's credit card. That's one of the benefits of age. This nickel-and-diming of Yvonne's accounts isn't going to work forever, but for now it should keep any creditors off her tail.

She should go home and get down to business, but there's no one to judge what she does or when she does it. Eventually, she'll have to get rid of the stubborn stain. Sooner or later someone will come to the house. Best not to leave evidence in plain sight. The chances of someone coming to her house are slim. No one but the occasional tree trimmer or religious fanatic has come by in years, so now or later is all the same— within reason. What she really needs is a do-over to get the business of living kickstarted. If one of those doors would open at the time she needs, that would solve everything.

Instead of going home, she pulls out on to Haines St. and turns the other way. She likes the particular blue of the sky and the fact that the worst of the Indian summer is over. It's still warm and the autumnal smell of leaf blower gasoline is in the air, but the wind has relaxed so that only an occasional gust stirs it up. There's something just the tiniest bit otherworldly about the way the light pools on the asphalt.

The tiger bells, tied to the door with a red tasseled rope, tinkle as Delanie steps into Hamet's Salon. There is no Hamet in the place, not this time or any other time she's been here. Hamet most likely lives behind some other door. One where this salon is a barbershop, or maybe a hookah lounge.

A chemical smell from a Brazilian blowout lingers in the room. It's just a matter of time before Delanie upgrades to a better salon. She'll find a good one in Studio City or even Brentwood. Maybe she'll start getting the full spa treatments.

Only Lily is on duty at this time on a Tuesday. She sits on a high stool at the desk, playing with her phone. She's wearing trendy yoga pants that don't flatter her, but her hair is perfect. She smiles when she sees Delanie. "Oh, honey, let's touch those roots up."

Lily, at no more than twenty-five, has not earned the right to call her "honey." It's entirely too familiar. Condescending even. Delanie wonders for a moment if this offense might be egregious enough to warrant an accident. *Now that's just being greedy*, Delanie chastises herself. From the way things are looking, she'd probably get away with it. But maybe it's best not to tempt fate. She decides to see how things go. "Is Kim in?"

Lily's smile fades from friendly to professional. "Just me."

Delanie likes that she got the tiniest of digs in. She could do more. The fact that she doesn't makes her feel powerful.

Lily moves through the world like her looks are her currency. Delanie knows the type. She prefers Kim, who knows what to do and doesn't waste the few words she knows of English on chit-chat.

Lily will do though. Delanie isn't ready to go home to tackle the mess she's got waiting for her there. She hates the smell of bleach. And if things go one way rather than another, her hair should look nice. There will surely be photographs.

"You want a cut too?" Lily puts her phone in her Kate Spade knockoff. She extends her well-groomed hand.

Delanie looks from Lily's professional smile to the red-leather chair at the closest station. In the space between, there's a shimmer of otherworldly light. A snap like a tree branch breaking changes the tang of the blowout chemicals to something entirely more earthy.

Yvonne, at the best of times, is over two hundred pounds. She, of course, never felt the least bit of shame about it. To be fair, she does carry her weight well. Or she did. As the first blue streaks of morning seep into the sky, Yvonne's weight problem had become Delanie's weight problem. Every time Delanie bends to lift her, the wind blows her shirt up, binding her shoulders and adding just that much more difficulty to the chore. Yvonne won't budge. This is not a problem Delanie had foreseen. She mentally kicks herself for her poor planning. When yet another heave fails to move Yvonne any closer to the pit she's dug at the base of the mulberry tree, Delanie drops her stiff leg and heads to the kitchen to get the good knife. Even though she's entered the scene too late to fix the main problem, she's not missing a chance to make the situation a little easier with this do-over.

"About those nails, girlfriend."

Delanie blinks and snatches her hand away from Lily's grip.

"That's okay." Lily turns away and grabs her case from the station behind. "You don't have to be embarrassed. That's why you come here, right?"

Delanie's nails are ragged and chipped. She hadn't noticed how bad they looked when she left the house this morning. In fact, she's sure they had looked just fine. She remembers thinking the ridges would need a fill soon, but they could go another week. As she looks at her manicure now, only vestiges of her crimson polish remain. Her cuticles are stained rusty brown where they've cracked. This is a new development. She suspects when she gets home she'll find an even bigger mess than when she left. That's not exactly what she wants to accomplish with a do-over. Maybe she should have gotten two gallons of bleach. She needs to be careful. These doors are getting out of control.

Delanie looks up. Her three weeks of gray growth is chestnut brown. The cut is easily three inches shorter than she prefers, and she's been styled in ways she's never tried before. It doesn't look bad, necessarily. It's probably going to cost a fortune. But that shouldn't be a problem for long.

Delanie wonders what her body does when she goes through a door. Does she talk? Does she agree to things that she normally wouldn't? It doesn't seem like Lily even noticed she was gone. That's the type of person Lily is. No respect.

The red leather squeaks and the mechanical guts creak as Delanie stands up. She's been sitting so long her legs don't want to move. For a minute, before she shakes it off, she catches a glimpse of herself moving like a decrepit old thing. The lights in the salon don't do her any favors. Maybe she should go with a lighter shade of lipstick. Something from Guerlain. Perhaps a lovely nude shade.

Delanie is afraid of the day, that will arrive sooner or later whether she wants it or not, when she's no longer able to shake off the stiffness. If she can just work things out though, she'll be able to buy herself all the new body parts she needs.

"Next time," Delanie says to Lily, who's setting up to give her a manicure. She steps up to the desk and pulls out her wallet. She flips through the cards until she finds the one she used at the grocery store. It should be good for a few more times, but not many more. Soon she'll have to solve the problem. Very soon. This haircut isn't going to be cheap.

"You sure?" Lily raises an eyebrow groomed for photos.

"Next time." The last thing Delanie needs is someone inspecting the dirt under her nails.

Lily comes to the desk and takes the credit card from Delanie. She glances at it, then inserts it in the reader. The machine churns out a strip of paper. She pulls the card out of the machine and studies it as Delanie puts the pen to the paper. Any scrawl will do.

"This says Yvonne on it," Lily says.

Delanie's heart hits her in the throat like a hammer. She nods like nothing is wrong, then casts her eyes over the desk. They fall on the letter opener in a cup by the register. If things get difficult, it would take relatively little effort to jam that in Lily's jugular. Delanie knows exactly where that is—now she does. Would have been nice to have that information before making a ridiculous mess. She's probably old-lady-invisible enough to get away with a second accident. Who wouldn't blame such a crime on the young woman's lover? He's most surely aggrieved, and everyone knows, it's always the boyfriend.

"You're not Yvonne." Lily says with that woman laugh that's designed to smooth the edges off words. "I know Yvonne. She's your friend you come in with sometimes."

"That's right. I'm not Yvonne," Delanie says. She's amazed by how even her voice sounds. The mistake people always make is explaining too much. Delanie isn't going to fall into that trap.

"Why do you have her card?"

Delanie has yet to land on an appropriate answer for this, but she's always been good at thinking on her feet. "We're partners in business." The truth. Every bit the truth. "Her money is my money." Also true, even though Yvonne didn't see it that way. Delanie can feel her façade wavering. A tremor is working its way from the pit of her stomach to her fingertips.

"Yeah, but I can't take this."

Delanie finds it disturbing that her hand shakes as she accepts the card. She can't make it stop no matter how hard she concentrates. Lily doesn't notice. She must think shaking is something a woman like Delanie would do. That annoys Delanie more than she wants to admit, but now is not the time for vanity. Delanie's eyes hone in on the letter opener.

"Oh, I'm sure it'll be fine this once," Lily says just in time.

Delanie glances down at the clock on her dash. **11:34**

Hell.

It's too close to the time she's supposed to meet Carl the lawyer for lunch to do anything else. She glances up in time to slam on her brakes to avoid running a red light.

A crash of thunder roars and rumbles as the interior of the Taurus crumbles away. The carpet is Delanie's favorite shade of crimson. Yvonne didn't even have an opinion about the color of the carpet or the paint or curtains or anything. She would have been fine working in a cardboard box. The red carpet has personality. And that's one of the things that made their mail-order jewelry business stand out from the pack.

Delanie sits down in the leather office chair. There's a brown ring from a long-ago coffee cup on the white laminate desktop. If a client ever came into their home office, the dirty desk would make a horrible impression. Delanie finds the sticky note she placed on the monitor to alert Yvonne to the problem. It had gone unheeded as usual, so she re-sticks it in a more prominent position. Delanie does all the work as it is. She's the one who gets the jewelry in stores and works the booths at craft fairs. It doesn't seem fair she should have to clean the office too. All Yvonne ever does is sit on her butt and push the buttons on the keyboard.

The screen flickers to life when Delanie bumps the mouse. The kittens-tangled-in-yarn wallpaper springs up just like always, with the little password box right in the center of the screen. There are six asterisks in the box. That is *not* the password, Delanie had discovered to her dismay. The symbols are only placeholders for the actual code. Apparently this is something everyone knows. She won't make that mistake again. Carl the lawyer nearly got bludgeoned to death when he gave her *that* look for reporting that the key to accessing the accounts was six consecutive asterisks.

As she shuffles through the used envelopes, canceled checks, grocery store flyers and pages torn from little notebooks that Yvonne uses to write down things she wants to remember, the door swings open.

"There you are! I've been looking everywhere for you," Yvonne says in that perky way she has, as though every sentence ends with an exclamation point. She tucks her asthma inhaler into the pack she always wears around her ample hips. The fruit-vomit smell of her gum fills the room.

Delanie jumps a little, but not so much as to look suspicious. She'd hoped to find the password and get back to where she ought to be without interacting with Yvonne. That was not to be though.

"What can I help you find?" Yvonne bustles over toward the desk in her no-nonsense way.

"What's the password again?" Delanie says, her voice as light and airy as she can muster.

"Up you go." Yvonne grabs the back of the chair and swivels it, and Delanie, around. She leans over and taps on the keyboard. "Success," she says as the guts of the computer spring to life.

"Let me do it." Delanie wants to scream, but she doesn't.

A car horn, maybe two or three, blares behind Delanie. The light is yellow. She grips the wheel of the Taurus and presses the gas. Inexplicably, the car goes in reverse. She's able to slam on the brake before she hits the car behind. Agitation surges through her and makes her tremble as she shifts into drive. The cars honk non-stop until she pulls through the intersection just as the light switches from yellow to red. She wishes she'd made all those honking cars wait on purpose. She'll settle for a happy accident though.

Delanie turns into the parking lot of the Persian Grill. Carl the lawyer loves this place. It's a little dimly lit for Delanie's taste, and the food is a touch too heavy for lunch, but it'll do. Soon she'll be dining in all the trendiest places. But for now, it's best to keep Carl happy. She needs his expertise.

As she walks to the door, Delanie laments the fact that she still doesn't have the password she needs in spite of all the effort she's made. She's locked in place by six stupid characters. She should be on a cruise by now. Carl better not act like it's some deficiency that only old people have. If he does that, Delanie can't promise that the situation won't get out of hand. She had pretty much risked her life going through that last door. No one seems to appreciate the sacrifices she makes.

Delanie is a little worried about how long she sat at that light. It seemed like a long time had passed, but she can't be sure. What if the police had gotten involved? How would she explain? She had vowed to be more careful. She doesn't know what she'll do if someone decides she isn't fit to drive anymore. That would be the end of everything. There'll be no more jewelry business then. No more anything except sitting at home and waiting to die.

Carl sits in a booth against the far wall. He stands up as she approaches the table. Carl is a nice young man with a receding hairline and a paunch that makes him look older than his thirty-five or so years. He's related to Yvonne, a second cousin perhaps, but there doesn't seem to be any familial love between them. He's not ambitious, which is probably a good thing where Delanie is concerned. He's practical and lacks imagination. These traits are all things Delanie puts in the plus column. He's not the type of man who sees things out of the ordinary. For Carl, if it can't be put on a spreadsheet, it doesn't exist.

Carl gives Delanie a perfunctory hug. He doesn't wear cologne even though a nice scent would cover the lingering whiff of dandruff shampoo that clings to him.

When the waiter arrives, Delanie orders a glass of wine. It's too early for cocktails, but what the hell. Carl orders a coffee and a plate of yalanchi sarma for them to share. So heavy and oily. Carl is going to be sorry he didn't choose to eat lighter one day.

"Good news," Carl says, pulling a leather binder from his briefcase. "You're well within your rights to make decisions for the business if your partner is incommunicado in excess of one month. You haven't heard from Yvonne?"

"I have not," Delanie says. How is it possible that one month has passed already? That's the most horrific thought Delanie has ever entertained. Time truly is slipping away.

This statement is entirely true. She hasn't heard a peep out of Yvonne. Things she says on the other side of the door don't count. Carl would agree if she explained this to him. Of course, the concept of "doors" is entirely beyond his capacity to understand.

"Now on the matter of the business finances, have you been able to recover the password?"

Delanie studies his squinty eyes, magnified by his thick lenses. A good lawyer would be able to solve this problem for her. A good lawyer would transfer the funds to her bank account without all this internet nonsense. "I have not."

Carl frowns. "Your business is managed entirely online. Yvonne set it up so that access to accounts and records are only available that way. We can, of course, go to court—"

"No, that's going to take forever."

And uncover all sorts of things best left buried, Delanie thinks.

"You're right about that." Carl shuffles the papers he's taken from his briefcase as though they have any relevance at all. "We need access to email accounts and inventory and..." He runs his finger down the list he's printed out. "So many things. Everything would be so much easier if we could just get into Yvonne's accounts."

"I know that." Delanie would like to get her hands on something nice and heavy. What use is he if he isn't going to solve her problem? "If I could just find the password to her computer this would all be so much easier."

"So you haven't heard from her? Nothing?" Carl squints at papers like the answer might be hidden there.

"Not a word," Delanie says.

"You know" Carl's version of a devious smile creeps across his face. "Sometimes older people..."

"What?" What could this milquetoast possibly know about "older people" that Delanie has failed to comprehend?

"Sometimes older people write down their passwords and keep them in a safe place. Could Yvonne have done that?"

Ugh, like it takes a genius to think of that. Like Delanie hadn't turned every place in the house Yvonne had ever had access to upside down looking for a hiding place.

"Did she leave a wallet behind, or a—"

Yes! Yvonne wore that stupid fanny pack—always. Why hadn't Delanie thought of this before? What else would her housemate keep in such an inappropriate accessory? Delanie had assumed her fashion disaster of a renter had worn the bag so she'd always have her asthma inhaler close by, but of course this is where she'd hide her secrets.

How could she be so stupid? Delanie is sure that bag contains the solution to all her problems. For an instant she thinks she might rush home and dig it up. But what a mess that would make. That is not the best solution. She just has to be patient. She just has to wait for a door.

The waiter comes up to their table. Delanie isn't hungry, but she's going to order anyway. She's decided on the shawarma chicken; when she looks up at the waiter to order, a blast as loud as a bomb rattles the very foundation of the building.

The Santa Anas shriek. A pack of coyotes howl in delight as they tear into a rabbit, or perhaps a small house pet who wasn't let in. Yvonne is in pieces, which have all been compactly placed in the hole Delanie has dug beneath the mulberry tree. The task is so nearly complete. All that's left to do is to replace the dirt. Delanie throws the shovel aside and falls to her knees. The task is unpleasant but there's no avoiding it. She paws through the gore and viscera until she finds a nylon strap. She shakes Yvonne's fanny pack free and extracts it from the improvised grave. With great care she stands, shakes off the stiffness in her knees, and places it on the wrought-iron garden bench. She proceeds to fill the hole with dirt. First things first.

The moon is low in the sky by the time she pats the mound smooth. Falling leaves and a December rain will take care of the anomalies in the landscaping. Success, she congratulates herself. This is the best of all the burials yet.

Smeared with dirt and other unspeakable substances, Delanie sits down on the garden bench. She places Yvonne's fanny pack on her lap, touching it reverently as though it's a religious artifact. With great fanfare, she unzips it and dumps out its contents.

Tension builds inside her. The door always seems to swing shut and transport her back before she gets what she needs. Delanie is determined not to let this happen this time. This time she will have success. She hurries to find her prize in Yvonne's hideous pouch, wary all the while that she's seconds away from being transported back to the table with a plate of steaming shawarma chicken sitting untouched in front of her. She unzips the thing. Plunges her hand inside. There's an asthma inhaler, a lip balm, a single piece of gum. She turns it inside out. Nothing more.

Nothing! This is the time when she's always pulled back. She's always returned when she fails.

But nothing happens. There's no sharp sound, no concerned companion, no event in progress that she has to navigate.

Why is she still here?

Unless... Delanie thinks. *I haven't failed. The opposite of failure is—success.*

It's so very obvious. The answer has been in front of her all the time. Delanie's heart patters with excitement. She'll be on that cruise in no time at all.

She rises from the bench and makes her way through the still-supple leaves blown free from the mulberry to the kitchen. Dust and debris sweep through the door with her and scatter across the tile floor. "Come on, door. Take me back. I have the answer."

She pours herself a glass of wine from her last bottle of 2014 Alexander Valley Cabernet. It's much better than the wine she ordered at the Persian Grill. In no time at all she'll be able to order another case. Soon she'll be able to afford all the fancy wine she wants. All of her planning and labor has paid off. She's guaranteed success as soon as she goes back through the door. And still, even though the minutes have ticked away and become an hour, more than an hour, no door appears.

S-U-C-C-E-S. Six letters. How could Delanie have missed something so obvious? She's tempted to go back to the office just to make sure. But she's not entirely sure there's an office at the end of the hall on this side of the door. And what if she encounters another door and gets lost in a labyrinth? That would be a tragedy after all her hard work to solve the puzzle. She'll just have to wait.

She walks back outside. The coyotes have moved on and the wind has died down. Leaves settle on the bare dirt of Yvonne's grave. The leaves bob on the surface of her koi pond. Her glass sparkles backlit blue.

Minutes tick into hours into a day, then another. Her shawarma chicken has surely congealed by now and Carl has moved on to help some other client. No one stops by. The world has grown so very small on this side of the door. She wonders what she's agreed to on the other side.

Time moves entirely too fast, but also too slow. As she's always feared it might, her world has grown very small. Delanie sits in the garden chair by the koi pond with a clear view of the mulberry tree and the secret that no one will ever know buried there as she waits for the door to pull her back through. She hopes it comes before the rest of her time slips away.